From PTA bake sales to sexy lingerie…suburbia takes on a whole new meaning

I pull into the parking lot of the nightclub. Neon lights flash C-20, my Friday night hangout from years ago. Called Café 210 back then, it went through a string of names like Ice and Bubby Jack's since. My hands shake as I turn the ignition off. Bass pounds in the background when I open the car door. I don't recognize the song. Damn, why would I? I listen to NPR. I take a deep breath and calm my nerves.

I never prowled for men before. Sure, I noticed, flirted, and enticed men in my twenties, but I wanted more. I searched for love and played at sex, which didn't often end in my favor. This is different. Now, I want meat. I am the stalker.

I step across the pavement. My heels click with each step and instill confidence, proclaiming my inner seductress. Sucking in my stomach, I push out my boobs and make a pouty face by pursing my lips together. In my mind, I imbue sexy.

My foot wobbles over a stone. My ankle turns in my two-inch heels. Instantly, in graceless motion, I fall hitting the pavement. I stare up at the starless night flat out on my back. I can't move for a second. No one comes to help me. Whatever.

I breathe deep, get up, dust myself off, and adjust my hair like nothing happened. A huge run streams up my stockings. Humbled, I smile at the bouncer and walk inside.

The Minivan Affairs

by

Jennifer Clarke & Anna Jones

This is a work of fiction. Names, characters, places, and incidents are either the product of the author's imagination or are used fictitiously, and any resemblance to actual persons living or dead, business establishments, events, or locales, is entirely coincidental.

The Minivan Affairs

Contact Information: info@thewildrosepress.com

Cover Art by *Diana Carlile*

The Wild Rose Press, Inc.
PO Box 708
Adams Basin, NY 14410-0708
Visit us at www.thewildrosepress.com

Publishing History
First Edition, 2021
Print ISBN 978-1-5092-3476-9
Digital ISBN 978-1-5092-3477-6

Published in the United States of America

Dedication

To exhausted moms everywhere craving minivan escapes. This adventure is for you.

Author Acknowledgments

Thank you Judi for taking a risk on two middle-aged, boring moms wanting to write a dirty novel. You made us better writers.

Chapter One

Anna

"Let's play," Jennifer demands without saying hello. Her keys rattle when they land on the metal table. I glance around the tiny coffee shop. College students slouch in the mismatched chairs, poring over textbooks or smartphones. At the counter, the barista chats with a customer. She uses too many *likes* in the conversation, and it grates on my nerves. Jennifer nods her head toward the new barista. "Her. Go."

I lower my voice so only Jennifer hears. "Her? Whatever. *Like*, I totally don't know. *Like*, a bottle blonde, career student studying for six years and still hasn't declared a major. She just hooked up with her best friend's boyfriend. Afterward, they *like* stopped at the grocery store and *like* ate a full bag of Cheetos before work. *Like*, it was *like* so romantic, but *like* don't tell anyone."

Jennifer crosses her eyes. "*Like*, totally yeah."

We laugh. The game is the perfect way to start our coffee date. In college, I noticed Jennifer sitting alone in the cafeteria and asked to join her table. I never made a better decision. If not for Jennifer, I imagine my college years plugged into a set of headphones and holed up in the library or art studio quietly observing life around me and not living. She said, "Yes, if you tell me about the cute boy in the red shirt, second in line."

"But…" My eyebrows furrowed. "I don't know him."

"Sure you do. Go." Her wide eyes studied me like I had a secret. "Try."

"Okay. A physics major who wears tighty-whities. Last night, he stayed up playing Nintendo, and his grandmother woke him for English class with her regular morning phone call. He'll eat his Lucky Charms cereal too fast and head back to his dorm room to defeat the Super Mario Brothers' boss for world domination. Thus, failing school this semester."

She smiled at me. "Yeah, for sure." In one goofy moment, our lifelong friendship bloomed, and we never stopped playing the game.

I inhale the roasted coffee scent, and a mindless smile grazes my face. The kind of expression that comes from parenting freedom. For the evening, I escaped the cries of "stop it" and "Mom," arguing about homework, making dinner, cleaning, bedtime rituals, and negotiating sleep.

I sip my tasteless lemon ginger tea and exchange typed pages with Jennifer. We arranged this date to support one another's writing careers. Career is a generous description of our writing as we haven't made any money yet.

I dig through my school bag and sort piles of schoolwork left to grade before I find my latest manuscript draft. I hand her a crumpled stack of papers. Kindly, she doesn't grimace at the mess and presents a miniature container from her organizer filled with office supplies.

She taps the papers onto the table until they come

together and binds them with a pink paperclip. "So we'll keep meeting weekly and give each other feedback?" She grabs her pen and makes a note on my work. Then scribbles something in her planner. I know she blocked in time to read my chapters.

"Yes. I think I need another rewrite. Let me know what you think," I say.

She hands me a pretty folder. I open to freshly printed, crisp white pages waiting for a reader. "Don't hold back on mine. I want real critiques. Don't spare my feelings."

"I won't. Don't spare mine either." I nod, encouraging her and hoping our partnership will help accomplish our respective dreams. I pour too much sugar into my tea. "Brooklyn failed math. She didn't turn in any homework, and the teacher didn't enter the grades until yesterday. Report cards come out Monday."

"Shit. Did you ask for a conference?"

"Yes, another conference at school with my coworkers. Whatever." I doodle a schoolhouse bell on the margins of one of the student's spelling tests.

"Ugh, it's too much to manage. I spent the entire day fighting with Kevin about going to soccer practice." Jennifer unwinds her multicolored scarf.

"Whatever. You paid for it already and invested your time. He must stick with it for the season."

Funky music plays over invisible speakers. I listen trying to understand the words but know it's a fruitless endeavor. "I need a change. I drag myself to teach each day and dread Monday like the plague. I'm not sure if I'll make it to the kindergarten graduation ceremony." No one listens to my random pleas for guidance. I fear the sage advice I crave doesn't exist.

"Fuck, me too," she agrees. She struggles as a stay-at-home mom without a paycheck. I pause a minute. Jennifer is the last person from college anyone would peg as a future stay-at-home mom. Though, she tried to juggle both. Right out of college, tons of big corporations recruited her through a headhunter. She landed a high-paying PR position with a downtown company.

The unexpected pregnancy didn't throw her off her game. She scheduled a C-section and hired a nanny. When maternity leave ended, her heart changed. After pumping in the bathroom for a week, she quit. Since then, she committed completely to parenting full-time. Now, she needs more out of her life. Hell, we both want more. We long to be writers, paid writers.

"Why is it so hard?" I twirl my hair and do not expect an answer.

"What?"

"Making money."

She smiles and adjusts her scarf. "Ever heard of the dinosaur porn books?" You can always count on Jennifer to steer the conversation somewhere weird and taboo.

"Dinosaur porn?" My eyebrows rise, and I stop twirling my hair.

"Yeah, people doing the nasty with dinosaurs."

"I don't get it." I grimace and sketch again. "How would it even work?"

"What do you mean?"

"You know, dinosaur's things are huge."

"Dinosaur's what?"

I blush. "Their, you know, tools."

"Tools?" She raises her eyebrows and smiles at me. "You mean dicks or cocks."

Heat rushes over my face. Jennifer likes to tease me about those dirty words. I can't say them and blush when she does.

"Who knows, dino dicks must be giant. Maybe it's part of the allure."

"Who wants to read about that stuff?"

"People obsessed with dinosaurs." She shrugs. "A friend sent me this link to an article about two young college students making over a hundred grand a year writing dinosaur porn books."

"Really?" My eyes narrow. Jennifer's lost her mind.

"Yes." She leans into the conversation. "So I did some research and read a bunch of popular smut books."

"You read dinosaur porn?"

"No, not that crazy stuff. I read romance books, but there are different levels of smut. Weird kinks, like dino sex, and then there's regular porn or softer stuff like women's romance fiction. I did an incognito Google search. Holy taco, there's a ton of shit out there. A lot of it isn't well written and people still buy it."

She rewraps her scarf with a knot around her neck. "We could write it with our eyes closed. One book I read was pure drivel, a sex scene, and back to more bullshit. Pretty soon I skipped through the sex parts because they got boring. How many ways can someone write 'he loved her so very well.' "

I listen as she continues. Her proposal baffles me. Is this a good cocktail story, or does she want to do this? Contemplating writing pornography makes me want to hide under the table.

"Romance books often publish with specialty companies, agents, and everything you can imagine. We'd need killer pen names to hide our real identities."

"True." I nod my head in agreement. *What the heck? She wants us to write an insane porn book?* We both sip our drinks in silence and give each other awkward smiles. We avoid one another's eyes at the prospect of writing erotica.

The conversation returns to normal mom issues. "Luke works late every night. They treat him as if he's the only lawyer at the firm. There is always some crisis he alone can solve. I guess a twenty-year commitment to a company and full partnership isn't enough to give him decent hours. His schedule gets worse each week." My teeth clench together, and I mark out my drawing.

"Jake sits on the couch, scratches his ass, and plays on his phone. He's home, but what good does it do me? My marriage lacks excitement. Jake stomps around angry but won't talk about anything in his life. He hasn't attempted to touch me in over seven months."

"Seven months? That's nuts." I pause to remember the last time I had sex with Luke. Holidays and birthdays flash through my mind. I can't recall a single time in recent history. "Feels like forever for us, too. He's never around anymore to do *it* with. When he comes home, we do family stuff: house chores, errands, take care of the kids." My phone pings with a text message from a colleague. "Shoot. What time does Party City close?"

"Nine. What now?"

"I forgot tomorrow is primary color day. I'm supposed to dress up as yellow."

Jennifer laughs. "You probably can find a yellow T-shirt somewhere in your house."

"Maybe, but you know how my fellow teachers react. They expect me to be covered head to toe in yellow. I need a yellow hat and yellow pants, too. Whatever." I sigh. "How's the new soccer coach? Any better than the last one?"

Our conversation plays through the little boring details of our lives: flu virus going around again, carpooling, making dinner, sick to death of grocery shopping, and on it goes. Under the mundane discussion, the idea of writing porn haunts me. A sexy tingle spreads through my body. My child-free hour with Jennifer expires, and I stop at Party City before heading home.

****

A thunderstorm rolls in as I tuck the kids into bed because Luke somehow forgot to do it. Idiot. I blow a kiss to Brooklyn and flip off the light in the hallway.

Thunder cracks, and lightning flashes across her ceiling. "Mommy."

"Yes."

"I'm scared."

"It will be okay. It's a small storm," I say.

Ben's feet scamper down the hallway as he runs into Brooklyn's room. "Did you see the flash?" he shouts and stands at the window to watch the sky.

"Yes, it's so loud. It won't last long." Rain pounds on the roof, and the wind pushes against the windows. "Come on." I sink into Brooklyn's bed and hold my arms out for them to snuggle. "Ben can sleep in here with you for tonight." They wiggle up beside me and under the covers. Thunder crashes again in the distance.

My fingers pet their baby cheeks.

I sing "Hush Little Baby" again and wait for them to fall asleep. My eyes droop shut next to their warm bodies. The storm passes, and the room fills with their soft breaths. I untangle myself from their limbs and the down comforter. Ben mumbles and turns over. Brooklyn dreams.

My nose scrunches at a putrid smell in the hall. I bet someone left a grilled cheese under their dresser or something gross. I make a mental note to find it later. In the dark, I plop onto my bed and something crackles under me. It's a yellow construction paper card from Ben.

He wrote "I mes u moomy" inside a big red circle.

My heart melts as I disappear into the laundry piles surrounding me. Lights from a nearby freeway streak across my ceiling. Luke shouts at the TV downstairs as the game drones in the background. He better not wake up the kids.

My phone's blue light shines on my face, and I text Jennifer.

—Let's do it.—

****

Jennifer

"Mom, I can't find my socks. Where are my soccer socks? Did you hide my socks?"

"Kevin, if you did your nighttime checklist like I asked, you'd have your soccer socks."

"Dad didn't make us."

"Just 'cause I'm gone one evening doesn't mean you can't follow your routine."

"Mom, I need the lucky socks."

"I'll keep searching. Maybe they're in your hamper. Did you remember to bring down the laundry last week?" I stumble over a stuffed rabbit in front of the washing machine. I'm gone one night and nothing gets done. My phone falls from my pocket, and a message from Anna waits for me.

—Let's do it.—

My blurry morning eyes squint. Did I read it correctly? She wants to do it? The text must be a late-night Hail Mary or a sadistic joke. I grab my glasses to make sure I read it correctly. Maybe Anna means something else? I read the text again. My eyes don't fool me.

—Let's do it.—

Holy taco, Anna lost her fucking mind for real this time. She can't mean writing porn. Anna continues to use childish words for fuck. She doesn't cuss ever. How can she possibly write a trashy novel without using dirty words? Hell, getting her to cuss became my mission in college. Once she said "tit" out loud at a party, and I fell over laughing.

Her writing porn equates to the end of the world. I grab my stomach and take a deep breath. She must be super desperate for a change. My thoughts fly to little details like organization and time management. How do I find time to do this little "sex" writing project? I shake off the idea. I don't want to get my hopes up. It could be a joke.

"Mom, where are you? Seriously, Mom, do you hear me? I can't find my socks. Where are my lucky soccer socks? Did you wash them?"

Keeping my voice calm, I say, "Again, I ask you, sweet child of mine, did you bring down the hamper on your scheduled day when I reminded you?"

I sort through piles of laundry, but my mind is a jumbled mess thinking about Anna's text. It must be a prank. When I proposed writing erotic junk or smut romance, I couldn't imagine kindergarten teacher Anna writing smut. Her corporate lawyer husband would be mortified if she did anything to sully the family name.

Making quick money writing porn could be the answer for both of us…well, in a warped, scary, I am a crazy-middle-aged-lady-desperate-for-a-life kind of scenario. Shit, if she is sincere, I need to engage in sex for this writing project to work.

Jake stumbles around the kitchen toasting bagels as I continue to dig through the dirty clothes basket. Holy taco, I'm overwhelmed by the middle schooler's stink. Jake pops his head in, and I lower my voice to make it sultry. "Hey, Jake, after I get the kids off to school, do you wanna go into work late? Maybe stay home and play?" I flutter my eyelashes at him over the heap of laundry.

"No. I gotta meeting at nine. In fact, I leave in five minutes. I won't be home for dinner. See ya."

"Yeah, okay," I say to his retreating back. Total rejection and no morning sex for me. It doesn't matter anymore. Last time we bothered with sex it wasn't eventful. I can picture the erotic book now.

Dear Reader,

My forty-eight-year-old husband ejaculated into me, grunted, "Thanks, babe," and rolled over to sleep. The evening of duty-filled married sex was over before I got aroused. His snoring adds more spice than his callused hands. Just an inspirational Saturday night of lovemaking. Sexy huh?

That won't sell many books. Our relationship wasn't always boring. Our frequent pre-kid marriage sex involved urgent fumbling to make it inside the house. We tore our clothes off in lust-filled passion. We were crazy about one another, or so I thought.

After the early spark-filled years fizzled out, we still scheduled time together creating an adequate sex life. The bedroom died a bland death when I didn't return to work after baby number one. I don't even remember how baby number two happened.

Jake took on a job he hated with a better salary and a ton more responsibility, stress, and hours. He wasn't adventurous in the bedroom before, but with the added pressure, it got worse. He never tries interesting positions, only face-to-face sex. The Kama Sutra and Jake don't mix.

Shit, how did my marriage become so pathetic? I don't look forward to spending time with him. I am certain he feels the same about me. Obviously, he is not interested enough to stay home an extra twenty minutes to fool around missionary style.

Falling into our newlywed sex-filled memories doesn't help me get into the morning mom zone. My shoulders droop. "I want to hide from my life," I tell the laundry. Instead, I crawl on top of the washing machine in search of soccer socks.

"Hey, I found one sock," I yell up the empty stairs.

"Where are my shins?" a young voice hollers.

"Third drawer, you know, the drawer labeled Sports," I mutter back, though he can't hear me.

The kids continue shouting and requesting items, so I collapse on top of the washer. No one else frequents this space. Here, the most depressing room in the house, surrounded by dirty laundry and clothes hangers, I find peace and text Anna.

—Can I leave Jake to start a new life? Run away from the chaos I created?—

I shove the phone back in my jeans pocket, not expecting a response. She probably won't acknowledge it, anyway. She'll know it's a hard mom moment for me, and I need to vent.

"Mom? Mom, where are you? I can't find my water bottle. I need that specific one. It's my lucky blue one. Mom…" I push the mountain of clothes aside and get up. My sex life before marriage seems far away as if in another person's memories. Will I be able to remember the uninhibited freedom I felt back then enough to write about it? I read chick-lit or women's romance, but I need to research more erotic work. Dirty stuff might give me ideas.

"It's in the dishwasher." I rush into my bedroom, grab my Kindle, and download as many sexy novels as I can find in the Kindle app. My eyes widen at what I locate beyond the romance section. There is a super kinky world out there left to explore.

I joked with Anna about the dino porn, but there are fetishes I didn't know existed. Most of them aren't strange, but a subgenre of their own: foot porn, tattoos and piercings for turn-ons, arousal from the sound of thunder, werewolf men, furries, and fixations I don't want to know about involving body fluids. I shudder at the last one.

Before my innocent search, I thought erotica was about sex, more sex, and sex in different positions or with new partners. Learning about this sexy time thing means more fun. Download complete, I bury my Kindle under the bed.

I exit my bedroom wearing a PJ top, jeans, a scarf, and my Louis Vuitton purse. "It's time to go. If you left soccer stuff, text me. I will bring it to the field after school. Gabby, don't forget your All About Me picture poster. I don't want to be late."

Chapter Two

Jennifer

"Where the fuck did I put it?" I mumble under my breath with half of my body beneath our king-sized bed. I squirm around avoiding the dust bunnies. With the kids asleep in the next room, I stop reading and take action. I need sex, and seducing Jake is my best chance.

Married sex implies a rote boring routine, but tonight will involve acrobatics and toys. Jake's head will spin. Our sex life leaves room for improvement. Eighteen years in my stable but now middle-aged and dull marriage will not pass as sensual on paper. "Shit, where did I hide the damn thing?" I shimmy out from under the bed and head to the closet.

For this evening's adventure, I wear an old, green tank top and my husband's gray boxers. "Is this sexy?" I ask out loud to empty space in our walk-in closet. "Jake, baby, do these boxers make me hot?" I crack myself up using a seductive voice. It sounds ridiculous. Thank fuck no one can hear me. How could Jake desire me in this outfit? I look like a librarian crossed with a leprechaun having hot flashes.

I climb on a stool to reach the top shelf of the closet. Gripping the wooden shelves, I try not to fall. I pat between each purse lined up on the top shelf. A mixture of cedar and lavender hits my nose. Unable to see, I fumble through a stack of ugly sweaters Jake's mom gives me every Christmas. I mistakenly grab the scattered cedar balls under the discarded clothes. No luck.

I move around searching for my purple vibrator and tangle up my purse straps. I pull each one down and rearrange them back into a neat row. Maybe the introduction of an adult toy will spark Jake's interest. We can spice things up. I need material to write about later. I doubt anyone wants to read about me alone with my ancient vibrator or my snoring husband.

My hand slides past an object. "There you are," I whisper, only to find an old art project the kids created for Mother's Day. Glitter and glue stick to the dick-shaped thing. Weird, one of the kids stuck it up here. On the side, Tommy wrote: *To my favorite mom. I love you. Happy Mother's Day.*

I cherish the phallic art in my hand and remember the pride on my son's face when I unwrapped his gift. I set it on my dresser for safekeeping. I'll add it to his art box tomorrow. My hand goes back to search. "I wish I could at least see up there."

My purple vibrator isn't even one of the fun sex toys with two arms or a dance beat. No soft rubber to imitate the real thing, and it doesn't smell of candy. I didn't buy the thing. My girlfriends, who know I never masturbated with one, presented it on my thirtieth birthday as a gag gift.

Unused, it gathers dust in my closet, and my thirtieth birthday is a decade long gone. I pause in my search. Did I give it away at some point? I doubt I donated it to Goodwill. I clasp my hand around another dick-shaped thing and yank it down for inspection.

"Success."

Hours later, Jake walks into our room and notices me sprawled out on the bed, without a book, waiting for him with a vibrator in hand. "Uh, Jennifer, what in the hell ya doing?"

"Thought we might play a little tonight, Jake. We could use an intimate product this time. Spice things up a bit? No lame, vanilla sex for us, babe."

"Very funny. Ya know I don't like nasty stuff. Why do you gotta be dirty?"

"What's dirty about using a vibrator?" I blush bright red. Of course, he thinks vibrators are dirty.

"Reminds me of the time you wanted me to dress up like a cop, as if I want to go and wreck a good thing with role-play. Ya gotta go and ruin a perfectly nice night." His monotone voice grates my nerves.

"I want to shake things up, Jake. I'm not satisfied with our sex life. Can't we do something besides the missionary position? Please?"

"Ya know how I feel, Jennifer," Jake mumbles. "Nothing changed. Let's go to sleep and forget this mess. I'm too tired to do it anyway." He crawls under the sheets and although I lie beside him, I am alone with my vibrator. I don't move. A few minutes later, Jake leaps up and grabs his pillow. "I'll sleep on the couch tonight. Ya want the light on or off?"

"Off." I toss around, tangling myself in the sheets, and turn on the vibrator. It buzzes filling the silence. I freeze and lay there like a fucking loser. I can't get my husband to fuck me anymore. In the morning, I'll text Anna. Last night's proposal was meant as a joke. No sexy writing happening for me.

Anna doesn't want to do this project anyway. She

won't have anything fun to write about either. She won't judge me for my stodginess. The smut project sounded like a fun escape from our lives, but it's a fantasy.

I turn off the vibrator and stash it under the bed. Flicking on my bedside table lamp, I grab an Erin Condren life planner and red pen. I tap my pen on the tablet over and over trying not to focus on this smut book, but there are so many various aspects of the sex industry I wonder about. I compose a research list, even though I plan to call it quits tomorrow morning.

1. What the hell are Kegel balls, and why are they fun?

2. How do you turn someone on?

3. Edible panties. Are they sugar? Do they taste? Are they toxic?

4. What is a fuckboy haircut?

I think of a few extra things I need to take care of tomorrow, so I flip to my weekly layout and add to it.

1. Finish the PTA insert.

2. Call the soccer coach about missing the game.

3. Make dentist appointments for everyone.

4. Get Spring Break dates.

A few hours later, I wake with the lamp on and the pen and planner across my chest. My alarm clock hasn't gone off yet. I roll over, pushing the cotton sheets off the bed, and stumble to the kitchen passing a sleeping Jake on the sofa. He looks miserable with his giant body flung in the narrow space.

I click the coffee pot on and wait. The percolating bubbles of water boiling fills the silent kitchen. I can't start the day without a hit of caffeine. The roasted bean scent calms me. Sucking down the hot coffee, I realize I should text Anna now and cancel the project before I wake the kids for school. I reach into my purse, grab my phone, and a two a.m. text from her already waits.

—Ciao, I have so many brilliant ideas. This will be easy. Can't wait to read your first chapter.—

I almost spit my coffee on the floor. "Uh…shit." I am the dull one, not sweet Anna. Okay, fine, I can do this. I'll fabricate a sex life. It's fiction after all. I sip more coffee and prepare the kids' lunch. Baby carrots rest in three little Tupperware containers.

In between different schools, soccer, choir, band, dance, and the other activities, I'll pop out a book about my passionless sex life. No, I self-correct. The book represents the exciting sex life I want.

Retirement plan A in action. There is no need to worry about my life as a stay-at-home mom with aging gray hair anymore. I will write about my dream sex life or the sex life I had in my twenties, maybe? No, if I am honest with myself, the sex life I wish I enjoyed in my twenties.

I press the container lids holding the sandwiches and place them into the kid's lunch boxes with my daily note. I missed fooling around before marriage.

Tonight, I'll put the moves on Jake again, this time in lacy lingerie and a nice and "clean" missionary position for him. Tomorrow, I'll write down the dirty details. "Shit." Did I give Tommy peanut butter? He hates peanut butter. I open the lunches and move the sandwiches around to appease everyone. I'll be an erotic goddess tonight.

I revise: it will be quiet, no-moaning sex the kids can't hear, but something is better than nothing. Well, sex if the kids stay asleep and Jake comes to bed instead of staying on the couch with his boxed wine and Netflix.

I saunter through the living room and run my fingers through Jake's hair. "It's time to wake up," I whisper into his ear and notice the beer smell.

"Damn it, woman. Let me sleep a little more." He rolls over, and I head upstairs to wake the kids.

****

Anna

We meet at the tiny coffee shop and the same barista tells me about the specials in a chipper voice. She strings *like* into each sentence at least twice. She sounds like an idiot. I smile, take my rooibos tea, and plop down across from Jennifer at a red, metal retro table in the corner. It looks like the kitchen table I grew up with. "*Ciao*, sorry I'm late again."

"Shall we play?" Jennifer lifts a brow. Even though she is Ms. Organized and never late, she never holds my mess against me.

I scan the room. "Him," I say, nodding to the male coffee baristo.

"Oh *him…*" She sing-songs this murmur. "He is nutty in love with the girlfriend he left back home on the family farm. He came here to make money playing acoustic guitar. Poor guy isn't successful because he can't sing worth a damn, with a voice like a barking dog. This is a side job. He yearns for the day they are reunited. Until then, he fucks the Chili's hostess two doors down in nasty new ways."

"Brilliant," I grunt my approval, digging through my teacher bag. I shuffle through Hundred Days of School holiday hats I need to cut out before tomorrow, my scribbled notes on book ideas, papers to grade, and finally locate the draft.

I lay crumpled sheets in front of her and glance around as if this were some secret spy mission. Is anyone eavesdropping on us? The place remains empty but for a geeky-looking dude in the corner who has eyes only for his tablet. My head drops, my leg shakes, and I twirl my hair with my finger.

She hands me her work in a pretty folder and bites her nails. We swim in unknown territory. The small talk about husbands, children, school, and jobs vanishes. We jumped down a rabbit hole together and land in a new raunchy universe.

I open the flowered folder to her multicolored Post-it Notes lined up in a tidy grid. If only I could bottle up Jennifer's organization and sell it in pill form, then we'd all be rich.

I dive into her pages, reading sentence by sentence. I attempt to stay steady through the naughty words. It occurs to me, I've never read an erotic book before or watched porn. Reading this might kill me. Each vulgar word stands out as if highlighted with a fluorescent pink marker, and I keep holding back a giggle. I picture Jennifer and Jake together naked and shiver. It's not about their lives. Do not picture them together in bed.

I adjust to the language convincing myself I'm not a prude. I struggle to focus on her story and doodle heart patterns on a scrap of paper while she finishes reading my paragraphs. Her lips silently mouth the words. She doesn't look up yet. I can tell she's attempting to say something nice but is unable to find the right words. "Just say it, Jennifer."

"Seems like you're…" she says.

"Making love," I finish, not wanting to torment her any more.

"Yeah, making love with your husband and his luscious pack, ha."

"It's lame and lacks passion like my love life. Whatever."

Jennifer returns the pages to me. "The concept is romantic but not sexy enough to sell in an erotic fiction market."

"I know it sucks."

"The problem is it doesn't suck enough, ha."

I laugh.

We both pause and stare at the clean white sheets of paper with black print, all our dirty thoughts just don't cut it. Last month, I turned forty and celebrated seventeen years of marriage. The last time I *did* anything with a man other than Luke was decades ago. Hell, I can't remember the last time we did *it*. And when we *do it*, it's more of an obligation than pleasure. I don't remember my last orgasm.

"It's as if we lack experience to…" I twirl my hair.

"To write about fucking strangers in parking lots."

A grin spreads across my face. Jennifer's delightfully blunt. "Yeah, whatever."

It's silly, but I hoped we could make this idea work. Bills pile up faster than we can pay them, and work is unbearable. Like somehow making an erotica book would be easier to write, publish, and make money. Facing our failing marriages and loss of sex life is harder.

"Maybe we need to create the experience in real life." Jennifer's comment hangs in the air between us. Is she proposing we *do it* with strangers to gather book material? I'm not that desperate to write. There is no way I could cheat on my husband. Never. But I can't escape the small thrill at the thought of it. A tingling sensation warms between my legs.

Regardless, I'm middle-aged and chunky. I glance down at myself and twirl my mousy-brown hair. For casual dress Friday, I wear jeans and a T-shirt that says "Read." Damn. Sexy left the building years ago. I stare at Jennifer gauging her thoughts. Jennifer could attract men with her slender body, long dark hair, and expressive eyes if she dropped the mom garb.

She sips her drink, and I feign interest in mine. "Babysitter," she says with finality.

"Yeah, I need to head to the dollar store and buy junk to count for the Hundred Days of School party."

We cram our work back into our purses, hiding them away because they're dirty and because they aren't dirty enough. I pay the barista, and we head our separate ways back to our families.

****

Jennifer

Walking onto the soccer field, I glance around until I find Anna. We plan to hide from the other soccer moms and exchange a new set of chapters.

My purse conceals a crisp new folder with typed pages of all my dirty thoughts and a lot of embarrassment. I know in my heart it includes seven pages of total and utter shit. The writing isn't clean or edited to my normal standards. On top of the irregular mess, the sex scenes were difficult to write, much less read. How many times can I use the words suck and big?

Kind Anna won't hurt my feelings, but I need interesting material so this doesn't happen again. Experts always say write what you know. My expertise at the missionary position makes for a short book. To further my education and word count, I consumed the downloaded Kindle smut as fast as possible. My new first sentence:

Dear Reader,

His big, luscious pack came toward me as I rolled over in my rubber dress trying to look seductive.

Yeah, it's total crap. My first sentence is a comedy of errors, and not sensual. Like any dude's package is luscious? Rubber dress? What a joke. Jake wears gray sweatpants and an X-Men graphic T-shirt covered in holes to bed every night. Nothing resembling rubber clothing ever touched my body in this rote, married life. There is no way I could squeeze my sagging boobs into rubber.

The soccer game starts, and Anna sets up a blanket a few feet away from the field. Her light brown hair frames her face, and her crystal blue eyes meet mine. I fiddle with my thermos and say to another parent, "I left something in the car." It isn't like me to walk away from a game, but I don't want any of the other parents to join us.

I pull my pages out of my purse and sit on Anna's blanket without saying a word. She smiles and begins reading to herself. Anna's face contorts controlling her expression. She scans the pages. I know her too well. She thinks it is total shit, again. Scrunching her mouth, she pauses contemplating what to say. Her eyes shift. "It's like…"

"Obligatory sex." Heat rises up my neck. I want to

save face with my friend. "Ugh, it's total trash, right? You hate it. I recall the last night I spent with Jake. Sex from seven months ago is hard to remember. I thought I had some wild moves." I laugh too loud and adjust my scarf. "I failed with nothing fun to share."

In a rush to find the right words, I say, "So okay, okay. Hear me out because this is bad. No, beyond fucking *evil* bad. I need to do new things and experience real excitement. We need new sex experiences to talk about, maybe new people?" I don't take a breath. "Like maybe I should, you know, hook up with some random men and then write about it. At least I'd create fodder for our book."

Anna doesn't acknowledge me.

"It's insane. I know. If I did it with other people, you couldn't tell anyone." I jumble my erratic words. Anna watches the soccer game, avoiding eye contact.

Instead of backpedaling, I dig deeper realizing I want to try. I am interested in new experiences. Anna will think I am wicked. "My marriage doesn't produce intriguing sexual circumstances. It's not Jake's fault. Well, it isn't only his fault.

"I fall into bed every night exhausted just like him. I don't do special things for Jake anymore. Shit, the man hasn't taken me on a date in three years, and when we go out into the world, it's to attend a fucking school event with the kids. Neither of us makes the time for one another to maintain our marriage. Ha, can you believe some couples schedule date nights?" I slow down to a mumble like a toy losing its batteries. Soccer parents cheer in the background.

I push on and embarrass myself further. "You know, sex rarely happens in my house, if at all. I promise, it's not anything people want to read about, much less try at home." I keep rambling, but I can't stop the train wreck coming out of my mouth. "I'm no *Fifty Shades of Grey* in the bedroom. Anna, I'm thrilled I read *Fifty Shades of Grey* before falling asleep at night."

"Jennifer. It's fine. I get it. You and Jake aren't good together. I can't remember the last time I saw you two happy, not like back in college. Do you remember how much fun we had together?" Anna smiles. "And of course, I'll keep your secret." Anna bites her bottom lip and stares at the game for a moment. "It makes me think."

My heart pounds in her silence. It lasts too long, and I can't keep from fidgeting. I want to shout, "What makes you think?" Anna's unreadable expression doesn't change.

"Luke works overtime a lot. I can't remember the last time we spent alone together." She sorts through a stack of wrinkled papers, pulling out students' work and placing them aside before ordering the rest by page number. She sets them on the blanket beside me. I snatch them and read.

I love my husband and happily lie there in bed with him. We smile sweetly at one another and caress each other's arms gently. He slowly kisses my cheek and then...

I yawn and hide it behind my hand. Relief washes over me. Her sex scenes are as inadequate as mine. I glance down at her work for a few more minutes to collect my emotions and figure out something acceptable to say not involving the word shit. What's appropriate? "It's like you're…uh…so nice to each other."

We burst out laughing, causing a few parents' heads to turn toward us. One mom with blonde hair and a turquoise sweater tied over her shoulders signals for us to quiet down. Anna says, "Brilliant, Perky Mrs. Perfect wants us to settle down."

We giggle more like silly teenagers. The aggressive soccer game keeps the nosey moms busy yelling at their young stars on the field. They won't pay us a visit.

"Yeah, go get it, baby," a dad screams. I look at Anna with my eyes crossed. We collapse in hysterics.

"Well, we tried. It was a fun exercise," I say after we calm down a bit.

"It was an exercise in something." Anna wipes her eyes and twirls her hair. The kids run across the field near us. Anna gives her kid a thumbs-up when he looks her way. "If we did it, could it be a complete secret?"

"Wait. What?" Holy taco, don't laugh now.

"Do you think you could do…what you said, and no one would find out?"

I pause and think about it a moment. "Why should they? It won't be a long drawn out affair, just one-night stand sexiness. I'll be discreet, so it should be fine. Jake notices nothing about me anyway."

"Luke doesn't see me either. Whatever. He isn't interested."

I scream inside my head trying to figure Anna out. She stops talking and dumps out construction paper and zigzag scissors from her Mary Poppins bag. She cuts shapes for the kindergarteners. The game continues in the background. What is she thinking?

Chapter Three

Jennifer

"Mom. One more kiss, please," my youngest one says as I walk back into his bedroom for the third time.

"We already did our bedtime routine. It is time to go to sleep." I bend down to give another hug.

"I just want one more good night."

"Okay. We're done now. Good night and I love you." I walk out the door and straight to the pantry where I keep the wine. I pop open the bottle, pour, and glance around at the kitchen in silence. I scan over my plan book. For once, nothing needs my attention. I poke my head into the living room. Jake snores on the sofa in front of some game on TV. I scribble on my calendar, "impromptu writing time."

With my glass of wine in hand, I sit in front of my laptop and stare at the cursor. "Ugh, I have nothing," I tell it, then close the computer screen.

If I fuck random strangers and share, I need to create a dream list of sex positions. I turn to the list section of my planner.

Positions I should try/Positions of potential interest/Possible yoga practice:

1. Missionary position. I got this one down. Thank you, Jake.

2. Doggy style. Do I get to bark during this one?

3. From behind. Wait, is that the same as doggy style? Do I want to be called a dog?

4. Woman on top. Woman standing above. Is that a thing?

5. Sideways. What the hell is sideways?

6. Standing up. Hmm, have I done this? Against a wall, does that count? I think I tried it in college. Could someone hold me up? Would a man be too tall for my short frame?

7. In the shower or water of some kind. Isn't sex always bad in the shower? Jake never could get the angle right, too slippery. How do people do it against the tile?

8. In a hot tub. What about bacteria?

9. On an airplane. Like I ever go anywhere.

My red pen hangs in the air. I text Anna.

—Help. Listing sex positions and nothing exciting comes to mind.—

—That's fun.—

—My regular vanilla sex doesn't leave room for any creativity.—

Will she think I am a total loser? I can't help it. I am stuck. Nothing else sex-related comes to mind. She doesn't respond for ten minutes, so I text back.

—Shit, my sex life bores you. It's years of Jake and his missionary-position-only stance.—

—No, it's not. Give me a minute. In a restaurant.—

—No more boring married sex for me. What restaurant?—

—You're right. Get creative. I'll call you when I get in the car.—

Twenty minutes later, Anna calls. "*Ciao*, you still working on your list?" she says before I get out a hello.

"Kind of? I worry about being lame. Plus, I'm sure one of the kids will wake up any minute now."

"I set up a date with Luke in the city," Anna interrupts.

"That's great. Good job, Anna."

"I booked a hotel room and got Luke's mom to babysit. You know how hard it is to get them to help."

"I do." I nod, though she can't see me.

"He didn't show," she whispers.

"What do you mean he didn't show?" I grit my teeth, and I catch myself getting worked up on her behalf.

In a steady voice, Anna says, "I waited at Juniper for thirty minutes and then got a voicemail from his secretary to order dinner because Luke's meeting ran over. I did, the food arrived, and I heard nothing from him. So I sat across from an empty chair with the fancy cutlery, dressed up, and ate my seared scallops alone while his beef stroganoff got cold. At least I got a good meal out of it."

My fist clenches around the phone. Why doesn't she sound angry? "Shit, he didn't call or even text?"

"No, his phone goes straight to voicemail. I called his secretary, and she said they are holed up in the conference room trying to close a deal on some big merger. Apparently, it went wrong at the last minute. I even checked with her first before I booked a date with my own husband."

"Shit, that sucks." He is such an asshole.

"It's worse. I booked a penthouse room at the Ambassador. I planned to surprise him."

Pain grips my stomach for my rejected friend. "Oh sweetie, I'm so sorry."

"I don't understand. You know we were so good together. He'd do special things for me, and we wanted to spend time together. Do you remember the Valentine's days he planned?"

"How could I forget?"

"The surprise trips and handmade cards? And the one time he did a treasure hunt with clues to our first date and kiss and…" Anna's voice cracks at the memory. "The kids and exhaustion make it hard to do extra, and I get his job is important but…" She pauses as if she's wiping away a tear. Her voice comes back strong. "It's been over two years since anything romantic happened at my house."

"Shit, I'm sorry."

"Jennifer."

"Yes."

Anna pauses for a long time. "Do you think another man would want sex with me? Since college, I gained a lot of weight."

"Yes, for sure. You still catch a lot of men's eyes when you wear your tight, blue sweater. You're hot and curvy with pretty eyes. Though, I'd ditch the teacher T-shirts saying 'Read.' "

Anna laughs. "I want to do it."

"Do what?"

"The book. I'm in. We will do, you know…*it* with other people and write about it, in the name of research."

I stay silent letting her work through it. If I say, "Fuck yeah, it might be fun" will she think badly of me? I don't want to sound too excited. "Will anyone want to sleep with *me*?" I mumble after a full two minutes of silence.

"Jennifer. Of course, you're as pretty as you were in college. But I'd lose the hideous oversized jacket you always wear."

I laugh, agreeing.

"Brilliant. Total secret? You swear?" she says.

"Total secret. I swear," I repeat her words.

"I'm home now and going to rescue the kids from Grandma. Talk to you later, *ciao*."

"Bye," I say, hanging up. My friend is a rock star badass, and I cannot stop smiling.

The scent of onions and Brussels sprouts from dinner overwhelms me. I should kill the stink. I open the top drawer of my desk and pull out sticks from my incense stash. I light two sandalwood ones, get up, and wave them around to cover the food smell, then plunk them into the dirt of a plant to fumigate the house.

Back at my desk, I hold my pen over the blank sheet of paper. I need a different kind of list, so I remove it from the spiral spine and rip up the lame sex position inventory into a million pieces.

Baseball blares on the TV in the next room as I turn in my chair to make sure I'm alone. I refocus on my task. It seems the books I downloaded in the erotic literature genre follow male character themes: the hot firefighter, the military man home from war, or the cowboy who never left the ranch.

My slightly offensive list should catalog the stereotypical people I want to fuck. It's my outline for writing this dirty book. Since my fantasy world needs a boost, maybe the list will help me get into the spirit of things. I begin serious research for my career. By making this catalog of men, I officially do the crazy dance.

Sexy Time Character Checklist
1. A total stranger
2. One of the dad friends
3. A utility guy in a hard hat or boots or something tough looking
4. A man with an exotic accent
5. Soccer coach
6. Father figure
Kinda gross. What woman wants this?
7. Married man
8. Tattooed man
9. Three-piece suit businessman
10. Out of my league hottie
Okay, who isn't.
11. A woman
Gotta keep it interesting.
12. A jock
Boring.
13. A threesome?
Could I? Am I open enough? Oh, it's just a list.
14. A cop or firefighter
Cliché.

I remove the list from my planner and fold it into thirds before tucking the paper into my wallet, a safe place from my kids. I'm off to a good start.

****

Anna

I inch out of the driveway into the cul-de-sac because there are probably kids around, damn, always kids around. I'm surrounded by little people day in and day out, either my own kids or a classroom set. The matching McMansions in nondescript colors were built for them and their zealous PTA member parents. I leave my two kids with Jennifer and drive into the city.

My car idles at a stoplight, and I fiddle with my new hairstyle. I prepared a week for tonight's activity. I waxed everything smooth and shiny. My nails glimmer in bright pink with diamond-studded tips. I can no longer pick up my car keys. I left my hair in the hands of a twenty-something woman with a nose ring and a bad habit of chewing gum.

"What do you want?" She smacked her gum.

"To look young?"

She laughed and bobbed my hair in layers laced with blonde highlights. She added a pink streak to the front. My children made fun of me for days. The kids at school didn't even recognize me in makeup or without a long ponytail.

I steady my erratic breathing as the car hurls past the lights of the city. I stuffed myself into a strapless black corset with laces in the back. It tightens in my stomach and pushes my breasts up giving me a sexy curve. I slipped into a string lace thong and clasped black stockings onto garters. A little black dress and high heel boots complete the outfit. I'm sexy. Round, but sexy.

I pull into the parking lot of the nightclub. Neon lights flash C-20, my Friday night hangout from years ago. Called Café 210 back then, it went through a string of names like Ice and Bubby Jack's since. My hands shake as I turn the ignition off. Bass pounds in the background when I open the car door. I don't recognize the song. Damn, why would I? I listen to NPR. I take a deep breath and calm my nerves.

I never prowled for men before. Sure, I noticed,

flirted, and enticed men in my twenties, but I wanted more. I searched for love and played at sex, which didn't often end in my favor. This is different. Now, I want meat. I am the stalker.

I step across the pavement. My heels click with each step and instill confidence, proclaiming my inner seductress. Sucking in my stomach, I push out my boobs and make a pouty face by pursing my lips together. In my mind, I imbue sexy.

My foot wobbles over a stone. My ankle turns in my two-inch heels. Instantly, in graceless motion, I fall hitting the pavement. I stare up at the starless night flat out on my back. I can't move for a second. No one comes to help me. *Whatever.*

I breathe deep, get up, dust myself off, and adjust my hair like nothing happened. A huge run streams up my stockings. Humbled, I smile at the bouncer and walk inside.

The music pounds. The place appears old-school but updated. Black walls and dim lights set the mood for something sinister. Chrome tables and chairs sit high around the room. A spotlight illuminates a black stage awaiting a band. The familiar scent of stale beer, sweat, and lingering cigarette smoke comforts me. At least some things never change.

I stare at the almost empty room. Why did I come on a Tuesday night? The party crowd gathers on Fridays, but book club night is an easy excuse for the family.

Still, I press forward, checking for a man to target. I sit at the bar and take out a pack of cigarettes from my clutch purse. I quit smoking over a decade ago, but I bought them for tonight. My younger self enjoyed a cigarette while drinking.

The bartender walks over and says, “Ma’am.” He points to a no-smoking sign. Damn it. I forgot the city passed a smoking ban a few years back. I miss the cloud of smoke filling the room. Now, that I notice it, I want to cower in a corner. A fog of smoke makes a club more intimate. *Whatever.* I sigh and put the pack away.

He called me “ma’am.” Damn, he’s gorgeous and young, so very young, a bartender requirement. A sleeveless black shirt with C-20 written in silver block letters displays his biceps with perfection, and his tall, muscular body wears his tight jeans well. I guess it’s the bar uniform. My gaze lingers on his dimple too long, and I blush. He’s out of my league. I order a gin and tonic and gawk at him while he makes it.

A band sets up. People filter in and cluster in groups focused on the stage. I sip my drink as my eyes gaze from guy to guy. Most arrive in pairs. The place swims with girls, chipper young things with too much makeup and perky breasts. A couple of guys sit together in the corner and drink beer. I can’t tell from here if they’re cute. Do I go over and make myself available? Damn, I want a cigarette. I twirl my hair. I need something to do with my hands.

The loud, heavy metal band starts, and a group of fans scream. The chipper girls hit the dance floor. Two of the girls swing their bottoms around on display, giggling. My fingers clench around my empty gin and tonic as I glare at them.

An old dude eyes me from down the bar. With his potbelly hanging over his belt and his faded Kiss T-shirt, it looks like someone glued him to the barstool decades before. My drink gone, I order another. I will need to take a cab home. Damn, how the heck will I explain the expense to my workaholic husband?

This is a mistake. I stumble to the bathroom, tipsier than I should be from two gin and tonics. I step into the alcove and crinkle my nose at the vanilla air freshener with an undertone of urine. The dingy, fake wood panel walls reflect the fluorescent lights. I squint my eyes. The door shuts, and the music dims. I call Jennifer and duck into the corner as the phone rings.

"Anna? What's wrong?" Jennifer answers.

"I don't know what the heck to do. Everyone is with someone in groups, and they're too damn young. I can't walk over to someone and pick them up. I can't do this. I'm too old for this."

"You're not too fucking old. Maybe a bar is the wrong place?"

"Who the heck goes to a bar alone?"

"You do. You did."

"What do I do now? Walk over to a group of guys and ask who wants to do ah…*it* with me? This is ridiculous. I'm ridiculous."

"Come home and try something else later. Maybe we can go together next time."

"Who the heck will babysit the kids?" I bite my lip and wait for her answer.

"I don't know. Maybe we can try the internet. People meet up online now, right?"

"Don't they get killed that way?"

"Like it's any different from hooking up with someone at a bar?"

"I guess you're right. I wanted to do *it* with someone tonight. I got dressed up, and you're babysitting. It was a lot of effort to get here. Whatever.

I'll wait an hour and drive home."

"Don't be disappointed. Just come home. It's okay."

"I'll head home in a bit, *ciao*."

I press "End Call" and turn around. The bald bouncer from the front door stares at me. I didn't hear him come in. He winks. I blush. How much of the conversation did he overhear? He's not ugly, but not handsome either. I want to run my fingers along his soft brown skin. Where did that thought come from? He doesn't smile, but his intense eyes lock into mine. A shiver runs through me. His muscles pop through the tight C-20 shirt.

I move to leave the alcove, but he blocks the doorway with his large body. This isn't safe, but…I smile. I shift to move around him. He steps closer to me. I extend my hand toward his face to touch his firm jawline. Have I lost all control? I pull back. He steps closer to me. I want to run my hand from his broad shoulders down to his small waist. I can't do this. My heart races.

He inchess forward, and I move away. My back hits the women's bathroom door. He licks his thick lips, reaches over my head, and pushes the door open. I stumble a bit, and he grabs my waist to stop me from falling. I melt in his thick arms and inhale his musky cologne. It reeks of youth and muscle.

He winks at me. "You game, baby?" he asks in a whisper.

I nod yes. I nodded yes? What the heck. How am I in a bathroom with a twenty-something stranger? He moves in after me, clicks the door lock, and flicks off the lights. My knees shake. I can't do this to my husband and kids. I should stop this. The image of me sitting at Juniper alone waiting for Luke flashes through my mind. Well, I have a husband on paper, not in real life.

A dim glow from the crack beneath the door spreads across his enormous frame. Uncontrollable shaking invades my body, and I bump into the Formica counter. It digs into my back. He leans his head toward me and brushes his lips over my neck.

I can't believe he is this close. His thick, strong lips press against mine, so different from Luke's. Goose bumps line my back. His large hands lift me onto the counter. My breath trembles as his lips touch mine, soft and wet. His tongue forces its way into my mouth, hard and strong. I don't do anything. Damn.

I need to kiss back. My tongue slides against his. Another man kisses me. It's so different. My body tingles everywhere. He pulls my dress over my head and runs his hand up my stocking legs. He touches the garters and flicks the elastic. It pings my leg.

"Old broads know how to fuck."

Really? Is that an insult or a compliment? He will be disappointed because this is one old broad who doesn't know what the heck to do down there. His hand traces up my waist and lands on my covered breasts. He squeezes them and moans, making me melt. I can't remember the last time I heard anything like it.

I marvel at those huge hands. A surge of energy runs through my body. I can do this, and he's into it. I tug the C-20 shirt off and slide my hand over a sculpted chest. He tightens his muscles to give me the full effect of his perfect physique and undoes the top button of his pants. The zipper slides down, and his pants and boxers fall.

I rest my hands on his smooth biceps and squeeze the thick mass. I never…ah, *did* anyone this strong before. He pulls down the top of my corset exposing my breasts, and his mouth sucks my nipples. His large man tool rubs against me, hard, warm, and foreign.

My bouncer's hands slip off my panties, his mouth travels down, and I moan. Damn, this is brilliant. Flicking his tongue back and forth at a rapid pace, he places his hands on my tingling breasts. He pinches my nipples, and the pleasure builds until my body explodes.

Fabric crumples as he fumbles with his pants to produce a condom. Tearing it with his teeth, he rolls it onto his ready tool. It's thick and hard like the rest of his body. He thrusts deep. The thick size fills me with pleasure and pain. I groan, loving the ride. He pushes in and out until he stops at our release and grunts one final sexy murmur. Resting his head on my breasts for a moment, he pulls out.

Snatching my phone off the counter, he flexes his muscles and takes a selfie waist up. I watch him redress his muscular body. He looks at me, smiles, leans in, and touches his wet lips to mine for a moment, then leaves.

Chapter Four

Anna

I rush into Denny's late, again. My shoes slip on the greasy floor, and the bright lights sting my eyes. Nothing should be this bright at night. By the appearance of the other weary patrons, I'm not alone. Their haggard faces soak up a night of drinking with coffee and pancakes at the one restaurant open after midnight. Jennifer waits at a table with coffee and fries. I say hi as my phone buzzes again.

"Damn. He won't stop texting me. Look at this."

I toss the phone down, and Jennifer scrolls through my texts. "What the fuck. He's texting you a picture of his dick?"

"Yes, every day. It won't stop. I hide my phone or one of my kids will see ah…*it*."

"How'd he get your number?" She frowns at the photo.

"I don't know, looked it up on my phone? Is that possible?"

"I guess." She slides to another photo angle of his erect tool. "It's quite big."

"I told you it was."

"Yes, but telling and seeing are very different."

I take my phone back. "I don't know why he thinks I want to see *that*. It's not like it's attractive or a turn on."

"So you don't like his big dick?"

"Whatever. I don't find anyone's tool attractive."

"Tool?" Jennifer says "tool" with air quotes and rolls her eyes. "You don't find cocks attractive?"

"I like what it can do but not what it looks like." I bite my lip hoping Jennifer doesn't judge me. "I don't want pictures of ah…*it* on my phone in the carpool lane. I need to delete them forever, no cloud backup or anything. Do you know how?"

"No. I ask my kids to do shit like that."

"So do I, but I will not ask my teenager how to delete a dirty photo from my phone," I lean forward and loud whisper.

"Point taken. Ask her." Jennifer points to the young waitress with the purple streaked hair and enlarged earring holes.

"Who? The waitress?" I grimace and twirl my hair. Jennifer can't be serious.

"She's young."

"No," I mumble, but it's too late because Jennifer takes the phone and calls to her.

"Hey. How does my friend delete these text messages from her phone?" The waitress leers at the phone and then at me with a smirk. I blush bright red and want to disappear using sheer willpower.

"Slide here and the delete button pops up."

"Will they be gone forever?"

"Yep."

"Thank you."

"Coffee?"

"Yes, please, decaf." She pours and drops two menus on the burgundy laminate table. The steam fills my nose with roasted beans. I toss my pages to Jennifer and delete the fifty text messages from Jay the bouncer. "I liked it better when I didn't know his name."

"You could block him."

"I don't know how."

"I'm sure our waitress could help."

"Yes, but…" I inspect the man's tool photo and delete.

Jennifer arches her eyebrows. "You don't want to?"

"Well." I bite my lip again.

She leans in. "You like the attention."

"Of course, I do." I blush bright red. I should block him and not risk everything, but I get a special tingle inside each time he texts me.

"Let's play. You'll dig the one in the corner." Jennifer smirks.

"The young guy or the old coupler?"

"Hell yeah, both of them. He isn't so young. I bet he's college age. Him first." Jennifer goads me with a real smile now.

"He just left his girlfriend at home because he crushes on our waitress. He comes every week in hopes of eating in her section. She crushes on him too and won't leave this job she hates because she gets to serve him every day. Both are too shy to say anything to one another."

"Geez, depressing."

"Yeah, it kinda is." The college guy crawls out of his booth. "But every night he pleasures himself in the handicap bathroom imagining her naked. One day she might join him." My face turns red.

Jennifer laughs. "Better."

"You do the old couple."

"Ahh, a lot of wicked thoughts come to mind." She raises her eyebrows and tosses her scarf on the booth seat. "The two of them met in an online S&M community three years ago. They aren't married to each other, but their spouses no longer care what they do. They just left the S&M party where they trade off using whips. She is the Domme in the relationship. After a night of rigorous play, they come here for pancakes and milk."

I laugh so hard I spew coffee out of my mouth. "Brilliant, Jennifer. You won this round."

****

Jennifer

Anna glows with sexual energy as I hug her goodbye. How did shy Anna take such a plunge into the dark sexy side of life? In college, she hid in the corner at every party sipping one beer the whole night. It took an entire night of coaxing and a couple of shots to get her into a crowd of people. She came out of her shell a little after her semester abroad in Italy.

Still, I'm shocked sweet, quiet Anna lived out an erotic fantasy and wrote about it. I'm proud of her bravery. "Okay. I am off for more adventures. Keep going and don't forget to write about them," I say with a cheerful voice.

I climb into my muddy mom-mobile alone, and the fake smile fades.

Dear Reader,

No steamy adventures yet, and this was my insane idea. Anna is brave to follow through on fucking strangers. This whole sex experiment should be easy.

But here I am, this uptight, middle-aged, graying woman scampering off to pick up a new bow for the violin, my kid doesn't practice, instead of screwing someone. I embody the walking cliché mom minus the sticker on the back of my minivan advertising the number of children in stupid stick figures.

I put the teen hauler in drive and listen to one of the kid's pop stations on the radio. "I was born this way," Lady Gaga shrieks. Really, was I? Lately, I obsess over the kids' school assignments, what veggies to make for dinner which they will actually eat, and how to get everyone to their events. What the fuck is wrong with me, and what is the nasty smell in the van? Jamming to "Born This Way," I wiggle my shoulders, finding the beat.

I roll down the window, speed up, and pass a traffic cop. I cross my fingers on the steering wheel and hope he won't stop me. A traffic fine would hurt our bank account. "Oh, wait," I yell into the mom-mobile. A cop is on the to-do sex list. Maybe I should speed faster, but I can't force myself to do it and drop to twenty-five miles an hour.

The motorcycle cop flashes his lights on and drives up beside me. With the window down, I spot him next to me. Will he pull me over? I slow, unsure of what to do. He matches my speed. Still, no sirens blare, just flashing lights. He stares at me. Wait, what? Does he want me to stop? He hand signals now, so I turn into the parking lot of a Baptist church. He follows.

"License and registration, please."

I look up at his young face on a tall, muscular body. Holy taco, I want to scream. A cop is on the list. I bite my tongue and fumble around in my glove box for the paperwork.

I contemplate saying something seductive to him about looking in my box. "Yes, sir," I say instead. "Did I do something wrong, officer?" Can I make a pass at a cop? It seems way out of bounds. I open my glove box and pull out the labeled envelope. My hands shake a little as I hand him the insurance and my driver's license.

"You were driving twenty-five over the speed limit. Be right back, ma'am." I undo my top three buttons and refresh my red lipstick as he checks my credentials in his car. He stands next to the window. "Your record's clean, no tickets or any other violations," he says, voice sultry, and his eyes linger on my painted lips and trail to my displayed cleavage.

He passes back my card. I reach for it, but he keeps his hand on the license.

"This mom van doesn't usually go fast, not like your motorcycle. I always wanted to ride one." I bat my eyes and strain to gaze up at him. Shit, what did I say?

"Yeah." He glances around into the back of the van and shoots me a questioning look. "Do I know you? You look familiar."

He lets go of the card but not before our fingers touch. "I don't think so. I'm not often in trouble with the law, officer."

"You can sit on my bike and test how it feels between your legs."

"Really?" My stomach turns. Shit, the flirting worked. I open the door and shift to exit the car but tumble half out suspended by the seatbelt. For a moment, I hang like a ragdoll in the air, not completely in the swagger wagon or fully on the ground.

"Have you been drinking?" He steps back and places his hand on the gun holster.

I squirm to get back in the seat and take the belt off. "No, officer, I forgot about the seatbelt."

"Please exit the car."

"Trying." I half fall out again but this time the belt is off. I manage to stand beside him. He comes closer to my face. "Have you been drinking?"

"No, I just got nervous. Drinking and driving don't mix." He smells my breath as if he doesn't believe me.

"Walk along the white line." My knees buckle, but I manage it without looking drunk.

"Not a sip of alcohol passed my lips tonight. I don't drink and drive."

"Well, good. I'll let you go with a warning this time. You should get home now. It is too late to be out alone as a little woman." He postures with authority.

"Yes, sir," is all I can mumble. I hold my breath, forcing myself to not roll my eyes. How dare he tell me to go home, and to think I wanted to ride his motorcycle. No cop sex for me. He killed that desire. I worry no one will want me. With sexist men like him around, will I want to be with them? This whole sexy stereotype idea is ridiculous, anyway.

"Okay, ma'am. Head straight home," he says again, not reading my face. Maybe he thinks he frightened me. I don't respond, roll up my window, and pull out of the parking lot at a crawl.

My hands clench the steering wheel as I drive through the empty streets. I can't believe my first attempt failed. So nervous I forgot the seatbelt. Fuck him, I don't want to go home. I pass my turn and drive aimlessly. Stranger sex could be the thing to shake the cobwebs off my coochie.

I need to jump in like Anna. No more made-up stories. No more woe is me scenarios and absolutely no cops. I crank up the radio. ACDC blares "Highway to Hell," but I drive the speed limit. No reason to tempt fate twice in one night. I need to start the naughty time research.

The song changes on the radio, and Barry Manilow's voice comes through the speakers. "ACDC to Manilow?" I say out loud and swerve the mom machine to change the station. A huge truck next to me blares his horn. "Shit." I am too in my head about this stupid sexist cop. I pull into a grocery store parking lot and dial Anna. No answer. Her voicemail answers. "It's Anna. Leave a message. *Ciao*."

"Anna, it's me. So yeah, driving around aimlessly, and I was stopped by a cop on Broadmore. I flirted with him, but he thought I was drunk. Like I would ever drink and drive. I am the poster mom for MADD. Though, I did fall out of the van. Then he had the gall to call me a little woman. Fuck sexism. I realize now I over analyzed this sex shit by reading about it. You jumped right in without research. I either need to do this or find some serious inspiration in Jake. But give me a break. Jake will never be someone different. I need to let go. I'm nervous. It's been a long time since I had sex with anyone other than Jake."

Her phone beeps. Shit, I forgot to explain the cop drama.

I fumble with the radio knobs again and find a country station. My mind wanders to Jake as I drive. I hate cowboy music, and he loves it, the more twang the better. A woman on the radio croons about her husband

and living in a state of numbness. "Fuck yeah, baby," I yell.

My knuckles turn white as I grip the steering wheel. We don't even fight well. Jake's so angry all the time. We are two people who share a house and raise kids next to one another instead of together. "We are so fucking different," I say to Reba McEntire on the radio.

I pull into the Taco Bell parking lot. I order a Diet Coke and try Anna one more time. Voicemail again. "Okay, you must be busy or your phone is off. An affair might be the result of my marriage dying a boring death, but really, it's about my self-worth. I need to feel beautiful and valued again.

"I am a sagging, graying, middle-aged woman who is never given emotional or physical support. Plus, there's the whole *I birthed a baby* issue. The sagging doesn't stop at my arms, Anna. My cookie is no longer a firm organ. And Anna, it doesn't matter if I do Kegels at every stoplight. Yes, I do them at every red light. Could a random man want me? Should I dye my hair and get rid of the gray streaks?" I rant.

I throw the phone in the backseat, so I'll stop calling her. The car behind me honks, and I move up in the drive-through line. "Yeah, yeah," I say and wave to him. I need to get over my bullshit.

Chapter Five

Jennifer

My mom deadheads the mums on our front porch steps. I bend down to stop her. “It’s okay, I scheduled a few hours tomorrow to take care of the garden.”

“Jennifer, you know if you don’t deadhead them, you won’t get more blooms.”

“I know. I intend to do it when I work on the yard.” She keeps plucking. “Are you sure you don’t mind babysitting the kids tonight?” Jake’s working out of town this week, so my mother came for a visit. She nods her head, yes, but shifts her eyes away from me laying on the mom guilt.

“I know it’s your first night here, but I must attend a meeting for the school’s PTA carnival committee. The meeting won’t end until nine or ten.” I lie, and a fist punches my gut. My mom suffocates me by following me around the house and continuously talking. Five hours together and I want to die.

“Of course, I can babysit, Jennifer. You go and do what you need to do. I understand PTA school board meetings. It wasn’t so long ago, I attended them, too. Though, I can’t remember them occurring this late at night.”

I don’t procrastinate a minute more. I jump into the minivan. Ugh, my nose scrunches up at the sour smell inside. I roll down the window to shout at the kids about leaving food in my mom-mobile but remember my sexy adventure plans. I back out of the driveway. I'll deal with the nasty smell later.

After the traffic stop disappointment, I crossed "fuck a cop" off the list and made another plan. No way will the cop stereotype equate sexy anymore. It's time to hit the out-of-town adult toy store for inspiration. This should be a great date night with the husband, well a husband interested in exploring sex. Not mine.

Every time I pass the store, I'm reminded of Jake calling me disgusting when I suggested it. Him making fun of me still stings. "You are so absurd. What if we got caught going there? Real funny, Jennifer. What if our neighbors found out?" I didn't respond. I will not let Jake mess with my head. Adult toy exploring here I come. Ha. Pun intended.

I bite my clear-painted nails and take a deep breath before pointing the mom ride in the right direction. I stop at a red traffic light. Are my husband's words true? Is this shopping trip foolish? When the light turns green, I pound the gas pedal. Foxy Time Toys looms large on the side of the busy interstate with an obnoxious oversized pair of tits blinking in pink neon lights. I pull into the parking lot as a warrior goddess.

A loud bell rings when I push open the solid door announcing my arrival, and I squint in the bright store lights. There is no way I can hide. I am here. I shrink into my winter coat.

After walking into the store, I catch a glimpse of myself in a full-length mirror and a frump reflects back. I can't believe my mother didn't say a single negative word about my appearance before I left the house. My body swims inside the puffy, poop-colored, goose-down coat. I look more like a robber on a stakeout than a soccer mom gathering ammunition for a life change.

My preconceived notions about this store were wrong. I expected a grungy space like the parking lot outside. It could be Target but for the graphic photos on the neatly organized shelves. Red, sparkly labels hang from the ceilings directing shoppers: vibrators, dildos, bondage, lubes, and lotions.

A clever end cap display says, “Things That Really Suck.” Another advertises the Womanizer. Light shines on a hot, young guy, maybe in his late twenties, in a white button-down shirt and khakis working the front counter. His tattoos cover his arms in an understated cool way rather than the *trying to piss off my parents* kind of way.

I zone out a bit and stare at him for an uncomfortable amount of time. He backs further away behind the counter. “Uh, can I help you? Are you okay?”

Shit, did he speak to me while I pontificated about the nature of his tattoos and idiot moms in big coats? Once again, not behaving sexy. I need to loosen up and head into this adventure appropriately. And maybe not walk around looking like an angry, soccer mom. I clear my throat with a terrible motor noise and blush. “Okay, yeah. Ugh, shit. Maybe?”

His lips form a smile, and he nods his head for me to go on.

“This whole sex shop thing is new to me. I am out of my comfort zone with no idea what I want. I need to do this, though. I must do something. Do you know what I mean?” I confess way more than someone walking into a store to purchase a few toys should.

He returns to the counter. "You don't need to be embarrassed. What brings you in today? Tell me what interests you? I am happy to help."

I raise my eyebrows, and he blushes crimson. I shed the coat, hoping to seem like a reasonable person. His shoulders relax as his gaze lands on my tight purple jeans and white T-shirt. His face brightens with a full-on smile. It's not anything special, but I roll my shoulders back and stand straighter.

"I think I want something other than a vibrator. It isn't unique enough to inspire creativity. What else is there to help you get going?" I trail off my explanation. I wish Anna was here. I have no idea what to ask for or what I want. I also realize the kids took my last two twenty-dollar bills. How will I pay on our credit card without Jake finding out? He will be mortified I came here, but I can't leave now. I made it this far.

The clerk gives me a come-hither with his finger and says, "It's okay, I can explain our products. Together we can find toys to enhance your play depending on the route you want to go. Then you can go home and experiment with your husband and find what works best for the two of you. Let's put a gift basket together, shall we? I can also suggest some creams and gels I like to use with my partners. I know you said no vibrators, but let's begin in the vibrator section to get a good idea of what you prefer. It's a good place to start. Many customers like the Bombes Clitoral Sucking Vibrator."

He leads me to a corner of vibrators in every shape and size. "Do you have a color preference? Handheld? Or perhaps a strap-on?"

I nod my head yes and hide my wedding band in my pocket. “Ah, no husband. And ah…and yes. I want to see it all.”

“Tell me what turns you on. Do you like traditional intercourse or is there something else you need for stimulation? Lots of people want to try new things such as anal sex. Is that part of the plan tonight?”

“I am not interested in anal sex. I mean, do I want to stick something up my hiney? Shit, am I too uptight?” I read his expression, but he isn’t giving anything away. “I want to try new toys, maybe something extraordinary, or find other ways to pleasure myself without a partner.”

He moves in close. I can’t help but notice his firm, long legs and don’t back away. The scent of pink bubblegum lingers around him. With a kind smile, he takes my hand and leads me toward another vibrator wall section behind us.

He ignores my anal response and murmurs above my ear. “I want to show you something your regular vibrator lacks. Wait, first, do you like your breasts stimulated during sex? Are you interested in clamping or cuffing?”

I flush bright red as he eyes my breasts. My nipples poke against my white T-shirt. I should have worn a bra but didn’t plan on taking my coat off in front of anyone. “I love when my breasts are touched, so that might work.” My voice hikes up a bit.

He abruptly turns and searches the store. Alone, I quiver. What is the plan? When he whips back, he kneels in front of me, and his hot breath envelopes my nipples. Only the thin fabric of my shirt separates his mouth from them. I almost say something about it being cold outside when he reaches for my waist. I tremble at his touch. My breasts nip in his face.

"Extraordinary. Are they yours, or did you buy them?" He gestures to my chest.

"Ha, my breasts? Buy them? No, this is me. One hundred percent the real thing." I joke.

Keeping his hands down, his tongue swirls over my shirt, making my hard nipples a sopping wet mess.

"Ohh, mmm," I moan a little.

He stops and lifts his eyebrow. "Very nice."

I'm not sure what to say. "Thanks?"

He throws his body against me. The outline of his hardness pushes through his khaki pants. He rubs it against my stomach. "Look what you did to me. Damn, those are beautiful breasts."

His hands work my nipples now as he grinds against me. I can't move, raise my hands, or respond. This is the first man, other than Jake, to touch me in years. Pleasure flushes my body.

"Now then." Back to business, he pulls away. "Let's find you some toys to get you as hot as I am right now. With those luscious breasts, we should head to the clasp and torture section. Nothing like a tiny bit of pain to make it more intense."

I want more. Is he done? "Ah, no."

He looks at me under hooded eyelids and moves to the other side of the store without a word. I follow. "Well, maybe the nipple clamps, but nothing too intense. I don't want any pain or BDSM stuff. I don't want vanilla either. Is there something in between those two extremes?"

"Of course, sweets. I can get you off more than one way." He grabs things off the shelf and throws them into a basket without discussion. “Let’s ring you up now, love.”

“Okay, but how do I know what to do with all of these products?” I stare at the hot pink basket full of items I didn’t know existed before today.

“I have complete faith you will figure it out. Nothing hotter than knowing how to please yourself. Don’t forget to enjoy the learning process,” he says with eyebrows raised and a quirky knowing smile.

I want to respond, “If you use your mouth on me again,” but I can’t force the words out. “Right,” I say in a weak voice.

Twenty minutes later, I walk out of the store with a huge bag of directionless equipment, a roll of colorful condoms, and some fodder for our sexy project. “Shit, Shiitt.” Safely back in the mom van, I exhale calming my frazzled nerves.

My wet T-shirt sticks to my skin so I waffle it back and forth, hoping it dries before I get home. What did I just do? I crank the engine and Taylor Swift blares through the speakers. The pop music shakes me out of my stupor. Shit, how will I explain an enormous credit card charge to Foxy Time Toys? I guess this is why people shop for sex toys on Amazon.

****

I upload coupons to my phone for my weekly shopping trip. The checkout line runs five people deep. It’s never this busy in the morning, which is precisely why I always shop now. Self-checkout drives me crazy. “Super busy today, huh?” I say to the tall woman in front of me. No answer. She turns and steps forward in line.

“Okay, ignore me,” I say to her back and peruse

the tabloid magazine rack.

I pick up a *Cosmopolitan* with a twenty-year-old model on the cover and flip through wondering when this new crop of celebrities came of age. I don't recognize a single star's name. I'm old. An intriguing article catches my eye, *Do Your Own Brazilian and Decorate It, Too.*

"Holy taco, Brazilian decoration?" The woman in front of me moves further up in line and sighs. Shit, I said that out loud. My face turns hot. I loosen the scarf around my neck.

I scan the article. A photo of a naked Barbie accompanies the text complete with glitter adorning her coochie. Spas now offer something called a Brazilian to wax women's bikini area and use adhesive jewels to enhance its appearance. I read the line twice, trying to decipher the meaning. Enhance the appearance of my lady love? Is this something I want to do?

This is out of my comfort zone because I am totally 1970 bush down there, loose and free. Do the other PTA moms wax and decorate their vajayjays with shiny objects? I should ask book club about it. But without copious amounts of alcohol, I won't discuss bush issues. "Ha." I laugh again. I could ask the lady in front of me about her personal jewels. Talk about freaking her out.

After the surprising adult toy store experience, I need to up my sexy game and will start with grooming. Like the boy scouts, I must prepare for new encounters. The article says, "Various creams and beautiful colored jewels require a different landscape for proper use. In addition to your trim and acquiring the right stones, you must reconsider all lingerie selections."

My mother and I never discussed the birds and the bees, much less how to maintain my pubic hair. I don't know anything about proper vajayjay grooming. Jake never mentions updating how my honey pot looks, but he never gets near it anymore to notice. I add the magazine to my basket for grocery checkout.

At home, I lock myself in the bathroom. I read eighty percent of college-age girls opt for the very popular Brazilian, a waxing where all hair is removed, even from the bum region. One spa alone performed 70,000 of them last year and expects the number to double. Why pay to look like a ten-year-old girl? Do guys like this clean look? How is it sexy? It sounds like extracting your teeth without anesthesia.

After five more minutes spent with the article, I still can't digest the information. Shit, there is no way I can do this on my own. I find a reputable spa offering this torture for women. The website states, "Before attending your scheduled appointment, you must decide between a chemical depilatory or simple waxing." To do this sexy time writing experiment I need to be all in or all clean as the case may be, but I won't put a chemical solution on my sugar cookie. I make an appointment for the next day.

****

At the spa, I find myself out of my element in the light pink bubble surrounded by the scent of eucalyptus. I never miss an appointment with my hairdresser, but spa days no longer happen, not since my pre-kid corporate days. Our budget no longer allows for it.

Soft classical music piped in from hidden speakers interrupts the silence. A sleek receptionist gives me a clipboard to check-in. The questions make me giggle.

"Number of sexual partners? When was your last menstrual cycle? List any sexually transmitted diseases." It is a bikini wax, not a doctor's appointment, so I only write my name and billing information. I hand it back and get a disapproving frown as she escorts me to another room filled with mute women.

The sleek, and now angry, receptionist deposits a heated robe in my lap and says, "Change into this, lock your things in the cabinet, and wait here."

When I return, the receptionist hands me a bottle of rose water. "Drink this for its healing properties." I smirk and she says, "Take a seat. Your clinician will be available in a few minutes."

I try to catch one of the other four waiting women's eyes. They sip their healing water, and I get no response. "Hem…hem." I clear my throat to catch someone's attention. Nothing. "So how about the game last night?" I joke. One woman frowns at me and goes back to her magazine. I give up.

"Jennifer?" I perk up at my name. Another woman in a white doctor's coat gestures toward me. I follow her like a baby duckling down a long, pink hallway.

"Hello. I am Sarah. I will perform your procedure today. Make yourself comfortable on the table."

I climb up and experience gynecological flashbacks. "Sounds fun." I lie down and thank the Greek gods for no stirrups.

She lowers her glasses and peers at me. "You chose the waxing method. Any experience with this procedure?" I hold back a giggle at her serious tone and bite the inside of my cheeks. I will not laugh.

"Nope. I am a virgin." I say to make her crack.

"I see." She lifts my gown. Her eyebrows rise.

"Oh, my." She frowns and says, "Wait. I need…give me a…hold on, back in a minute." She sprints out of the tiny room.

Unsure of what to do, I lie back on the table and close my eyes. The fluorescent lights buzz above me.

"Jennifer?" I startle. Holy taco, she snuck back into the room without a sound. "I need an assistant today with your procedure so it all goes well."

"Assistance?" A Spidey sense tingles up my spine.

"Yes."

In walks the largest, blondest woman ever to walk the face of the earth. "Hello there. My name is Olga." She pushes my gown aside. "Oh, I see."

"Olga? Where is your beautiful accent from?" I butter up the new assistant. My hands tremble at my side.

"I am Russian. Please lie back. I will count to ten. I don't want you to move. Yes?"

"I see. Yes?" I question back like a parrot.

Sarah stands next to me. Her hands hover near my stomach as if she might need to push me down. I tense.

Heat seeps onto my skin as Olga smears the hot wax, then more. Frantic whipping noises fill the room like Olga's an angry baker on a deadline. She returns with a wooden wand and leans down again on my honey pot with a grunt. More heat spreads across my pubic area. "Yes, well. Pull back a bit here. Yes, a little on the left," Olga instructs.

"Everything okay down there?" I ask, closing my eyes now.

"And three," Olga shouts as my entire body comes off the table along with all my 1970's hair in blinding pain.

****

Next thing I know, I find myself sprawled out on the gyno table in a fluffy, pink robe. It takes me a minute to figure out I am not in a doctor's office. Olga's gone, and Sarah perches on a chair in the corner.

"Yeah, you passed out," she says with one eyebrow cocked. "First for me."

Chapter Six

Anna

After standing in the rain for ten minutes, water pours down my body and soaks into my clothing. I shiver and not from the cold. I shut my keys in my car and lock the doors on purpose. My spare set waits in my purse, but I pretend to forget for now. The evening darkens over the empty parking lot. Blurred-red taillights of passing cars reflect in the muddy puddles. I return to the coffee shop's front door and knock.

He shakes his head and points to his watch. I don't leave. His tall body moves toward the door, and he seems to recognize me from earlier when I spent an hour sipping a giant cappuccino while pretending to write on my computer.

I come often, mostly with the family for after school treats or when I forget to make cookies for the PTA fundraisers. Near the school, the place caters to parents searching for a quick snack and a caffeine hit before carting their offspring to the next activity. It swarms with children in leotards or soccer cleats. My kids grew up eating their pinwheels and sugar cookies.

The new, sexy baristo caused a gossip storm during the school carpool. "Did you hear? He lives in the apartment above the shop. Yes, he's an artist. He painted the new abstract work on the walls." And the biggest news so far, “Someone said his more realistic pieces are not suitable for the general public. Lewd paintings.”

He answers the door. “Ms. Jones. I’m sorry. I didn’t recognize you for a moment. What’s wrong?”

“I locked myself out of my car.”

“Oh no.” He steps out into the rain. Large drops of water hit his white T-shirt as he walks around the car peeking through the windows. His hand pushes a loose strand of hair back over his ear and fixes his ponytail. “Sorry, but these new cars are impossible to get into now.”

“I called roadside service.” I lie and bite my bottom lip.

“Come in out of the rain until they get here.”

We dart back into the shop. Closed and dark, the place transforms into a forbidden chamber. The white cotton sticks to his skin and shows his muscular form.

“No problem. I can wait outside. They said it will take an hour or more. Too many accidents because of the weather.”

“No, don’t think of it. I’m finished here. Do you want to wait upstairs in my apartment? You can see the parking lot from my front window and get out of the rain.”

“Brilliant.” My voice hikes up too high. Damn. I follow him out the back through the kitchen. He turns off the last light and sets the alarm. We climb a metal staircase to his apartment and step into a dark room. I can’t believe I am here.

I should go home to my kids and husband. This is not like me. Where did this tiger woman come from? His arm glides past me to flick on the light. I linger close and inhale his scent. Nothing commercial like cologne, but a hint of body musk mixed with oil paint and coffee.

Large, bold, erotic paintings of female parts cover the walls of his apartment from floor to ceiling—breasts, vajayjays, legs. He grabs a kitchen towel and dries his face. The wet T-shirt slides off his lean body. I bite my lip as my gaze travels the small line of hair from his belly button down to his waist.

Rings decorate his nipples and tattoos cover his firm arms. I itch to trace them with my fingers but hold back. He grabs a flannel from the floor and pulls it over his head. Wet, wavy hair falls out of the ponytail and lands on his shoulders. I melt.

He picks up another one and says, "You look cold. You can wear this, and I'll throw yours in the dryer."

"Okay." I move closer and take the button-down shirt. I turn and tuck my hair to the side. "Could you?" I brazenly flirt unlike ever before.

Warm hands touch my neck as he slides down the zipper. Long fingers tingle my skin. I spin back and make a choice. This could count as the most embarrassing moment of my life or the best.

I step out of my dress and reveal all of me to this young, cute, punk artist. Jennifer used to hide my headphones and doctor me up with a shot of tequila before going to a party in college. Now, I bare myself before a young hottie who can't be interested in me. Whatever.

I wear my best stockings with a garter belt and lace corset. Careful not to catch his eye, I slip on the dress shirt and take my time buttoning it up. His gaze pierces into me with an unreadable expression.

In a sudden burst of energy, he says, "Perfect. Can you sit?" He pulls up an antique office chair on caster wheels.

I settle on the hard, wooden seat. Am I really doing this?

"Perfect. Will you pose for me? Centerpiece material."

"All right." My eyebrows knit together.

He brushes my hair. Warm hands caress my face. My entire body throbs. He adjusts me like a doll. His fingers unbutton the lower half of my shirt. Hands part my legs open. My lungs gasp for air. On his knees, before me, he says, "May I?" He clutches the side of my panties. I nod yes as he pulls them down to my knees exposing my *everything*. One arm rests on the chair, and the other touches my private place. He rummages through a drawer and return with a silver vibrator. A vibrator. I never. He sets it against my lady part but does not turn it on.

"Perfect. Can you hold the position?"

I nod. What the heck did I do? I'm a mom. A married mom. A married mom with cellulite. A married mom with cellulite covered thighs letting a stranger paint my *you know what*.

He arranges his easel and draws in feverish motions. The pencil scratches against the paper. I remain frozen, unable to breathe. Intense blue eyes stare at me and begin work again. I tremble. This is unreal.

The knob turns and the door opens. I jump. "Don't worry it's only Jessica, my girlfriend." Girlfriend? What the heck. I move to get up. "Please don't. This is perfect. I won't take much longer with this pose."

"Hey." She kisses him on the mouth. Why am I

still here? "Wow." She stops and gawks at me.

"I know. It's perfect. This is Mrs. Jones."

"It's like she's a regular woman. Maybe a mom on the outside but inside she's all sex. Wow. I brought Chinese. You hungry?"

"Not now. I need to focus." His eyes don't follow her but flick between me and his easel.

"What about you, Mrs. Jones?" The scent of patchouli greets me as she steps closer.

"*Ciao*, I'm Anna." I need less formality with my stuff hanging out in front of the world. I want to hide in a corner with my headphones and a sketchpad.

"Anna, you hungry? He takes forever. Drawing. Sex, too." She laughs between bites of Chinese food. "Oh dear, she's shaking. Are you cold?"

"No."

"Nervous? Don't be. He's talented. It will blow your mind when you see it." She takes an eggroll from the small takeout box with her fingers and places it under my nose. "Want some?" Long, blonde hair slides down her shoulders.

Her big eyes stare at me as she holds it up to my mouth like one does for an infant. I take a bite. This is too damn weird. Plum sauce invades my tongue as she feeds the rest to me before sauntering across the room. Jessica's body looks like every movie star on the big screen with a thin waist and long legs. My fists clench as I observe her every move.

I was never on her level of pretty. More than gorgeous, she knows sexy and every move she makes flaunts it. The TV blares *The Simpsons*, and she flops on the couch but manages to angle her body in a sensual way. The scene looks like a pinup magazine designed to sell eggrolls.

"Stop, please, you're a distraction." His hand waves to dismiss her and the TV.

"Okay fine." Jessica turns it off and flutters around the apartment eating Chinese noodles with her fingers. But damn it, she licks her fingers and somehow makes it provocative.

"Jessica, stop," he scolds her like a child.

"Okay. Okay. I'm out. Text me when you're done. I'll hang at Ricky's. Nice to meet you, Anna." She winks at me.

"*Ciao*." I frown. The apartment door slams shut.

"Better." He exhales a breath of air and pulls out his ponytail. Hair falls around his shoulders in golden brown waves. "She's ADHD nervous energy all the time. I can't work with her around. I finished the sketch, but I need your facial expression."

"My face?"

The pencil clicks, and he strides toward me. My breath lodges in my throat. His body hovers over me. He kneels and glides his hands up my legs, over my waist, and rests them on my tender breasts. I'm a complete puddle on the hardwood floor. His hand squeezes as his face closes in on my stuff an inch away.

His warm breath touches my skin as he waits. I moan, unable to control myself. Moments pass and tension builds. At last, his tongue licks my area. Moans explode from my mouth and bounce off the walls. His invasion continues. My body goes limp as the pleasure builds. The vibrator hums, and I jump from the intensity.

Hands hold it in place and rhythmically lift it on and off. My body sings with satisfaction. I open my eyes. He gazes back, memorizing my expression. I surrender to the arousal. "Please don't stop," I hum. Ever. I orgasm.

A perfect smile forms across his face, and his body presses on mine. His lips touch my lips. Gentle. Soft. He stands up, takes my hand, and leads me to his bed.

"What about Jessica?"

"She won't come back for a while. She knows. She teases guys at the bar, a favorite pastime. Sometimes they get lucky but not often."

I lay on my back, and he unbuttons the rest of my shirt. Pants and boxers drop to the hardwood floor. Wetness builds as I gaze at the young specimen of perfection. He leans in and licks my nipples as his hands slip up and down my body. A smear of paint from his stained hand caresses my waist. He tries in vain to wipe it off.

"Sorry. I painted you for real now." His face hints at a smile, and his eyes gaze down.

Damn, he's adorable. "Whatever." Nothing could bother me. He fumbles in a drawer beside the bed. A condom package tears open, and it slides on his tool. Where do I move my hands? They seem out of place. I rest them at my side to stop them from trembling. He moves his body on top of me. His knees straddle my straight legs as his body rubs against mine. He presses his chest into me, and he slides my legs apart. Kisses fill my neck. His hard tool grinds in my area.

What should I do with my hands? I ponder until he enters me. I cry out and scratch his back. He thrusts inside me at a higher angle than I'm accustomed to which makes his tool rub me in a perfect way. Pressure builds. He uses his hands to attack my aching breasts, squeezing and tugging. He yells, loud and unencumbered. I want to stay in this moment forever and unexpectedly orgasm, again. Two times in one day, a record for me.

Now, his eyes close and his lips pinch down. An intense groan escapes his body, and he collapses on me. My hands graze up his leg, his butt, his smooth back. He is perfect, all young muscle. He kisses my neck and touches my face. His eyes linger, and his softness surprises me.

"Do you want to see it?"

It takes me a minute to remember. "The painting?"

"Yes." His eyes cast downward. He stands up and wrings his hands fidgeting.

"Of course." I can't believe he's nervous.

His gentle hand reaches out to lead me to it. I become aware of my nakedness, especially my bare cellulite and fat lumps. Do I want my body memorialized in a work of art? I stare at a drawn image of me. His hands squeeze my waist, and the warmth of his body crushes against my back.

The canvas is me. Though, I never saw my body like this before. My face flushes with heat. The drawing shows me with almost closed eyes, a pursed mouth with my tongue touching my top lip. The oil color pallet sitting on the easel captures my complexion.

This creates a problem. Most of the lady part paintings in the apartment show no likeness to anyone specific. I didn't expect the canvass to contain my resemblance, something my husband or kids could recognize. Damn. I can't imagine anyone looking at this painting. I take a deep breath. No one I know will see it. Right?

"What do you think?" he asks.

"It's me. I didn't expect it to look like me."

"Yes, you're an inspiration. It will be the centerpiece of my show."

"Show. What show?" Damn, damn, damn.

"My work will be on exhibit at the Red Roof Wine Bar soon."

"But people will see me." I pull away from his embrace. "Nude me. My husband. My family. Damn, what did I do?"

He pulls me back. "My muse, it's beautiful art."

"But…" He stops my words with a searing hot kiss. He leans his body into mine, and somehow, I radiate more beauty than a fit twenty-year-old. I don't want to leave this fantasy, nor confront its new reality.

"I really should go."

"Stay. Take a shower with me."

I can't resist his perfection. Why is he interested in me? I follow him to the small bathroom. Hot water runs over our nakedness. His hard body clings onto mine. His hands rub me down, and I slip mine onto his huge package.

He kneels in the shower and licks me with his tongue. I need him inside me again. My nails dig into his shoulders, and the pleasure intensifies so much it hurts. My body becomes limp as I orgasm, and a loud yelp escapes my lips.

He pauses to get a condom. His body pins me against the shower wall, and I surrender. I succumb to a haze of fog, water, warmth, his strong body thrusting into mine, soft murmurs, and pleasure. I return to my senses in his bed, damp, naked, and beside him.

"Damn, I gotta get home. What time is it?"

****

I stumble into the diner late with an overflowing handbag. Jennifer waits at our favorite booth.

"Game first today. Go." She points at a man and swings a sparkly scarf around her neck.

I throw a handful of crumpled pages at Jennifer. "No, I can't. This isn't good." I ducked out of a professional development day and begged Jennifer to rearrange her calendar to meet me.

"Wait. What's wrong with it?"

"Read it. You'll understand between wiener pictures from the bouncer and this art show fiasco. Damn, I'm in trouble. Luke will find out." I plop down onto the vinyl booth.

"Why? What happened?" Her eyebrows raise as she straightens the stack of papers.

"Read," I demand.

Jennifer's eyes scan my scene with the baristo. She flips through each page and tension mounts.

"Shit, Anna, this is hot."

"Coffee and french fries please," I say to the waiter. "The same for her." Jennifer nods toward me. She always orders a salad to keep on her program, but I know she counts on me to break her dull food routine. This is our favorite greasy spoon. The coffee sucks, but the fries are brilliant. She leans forward over the table. "You fucked him twice and had three orgasms?"

"Art exhibit, focus on the art exhibit." I pound my fist down.

"Okay, I hear you, but impressive three-in-one escapade."

"Art show, Jennifer."

"How much does it look like you?"

The waiter pours coffee into our cups. I add three sugars, cream, and stir. "Completely like me. Like a damn photograph."

She sips her black coffee. Always the health nut, though even she can't resist Mozzy's fries. "Well, who will attend some barista's art show?"

My eyes widen. "Everyone we know. And it's baristo for a man. Barista for a woman."

"Thanks for the Italian lesson."

"Sorry. You know my Italian love runs deep."

"I get it. If I spent a semester in Italy, I'd hold on to it forever, too. Plus, I love your cultural tidbits."

"My heart will always belong to Italy but back to the topic."

"I'm sure no one will go to some *baristo's* show." She smiles at me, about to laugh.

"At book club…"

"Hold up. You go to book club now?" Jennifer blurts out.

I give her a mom stare. "At book club, they couldn't stop talking about the new baristo who paints naughty pictures. They will go. And if book club attends, my life is over."

"I'm sure if you ask the coffee guy in a nice way, he won't put the painting in the show."

The waiter drops the fries and the bill onto the table. Mozzy's isn't known for their service.

"No. Apparently, it's his masterpiece, the star of the whole show."

"Really?" she says and chucks a hot fry into her mouth.

"Don't act so surprised."

"I just mean, you know you're older and…"

"And what?"

"You know what I mean. We aren't spring chickens."

"Whatever. It's some damn statement about normalizing sexuality. Heck, I don't understand. Maybe soccer mom is horny or some such thing? If I expected the guy to paint a realistic image of me and show it to the public, I wouldn't have done *it* with him." I twirl my hair.

"Maybe no one will believe it's you." She adjusts her scarf.

"Seriously, what should I do?"

"I don't know." She sobers up. "This is bad and so fucking good, too. We can fix this."

"I don't know how to finish this sex book either. I can't pick anyone up at the club because the salami picture man works there. And now I can't even go to the coffee shop. I'm in serious trouble, and I already came this far."

"Dick pics," Jennifer says with a mouth full of fries.

"What?"

"That's what they call them. Dick pics. The Guardian had an article about them last July. It's a big problem."

"Fine, Ms. Cool Mom, good job keeping up with the kid's lingo. I can't go to the club again because my bouncer, king of the tool pics, works there."

Her mouth quirks. "How was the sex with the baristo? Did you at least enjoy it?"

She loves this debacle.

I smile. "Yes, it was brilliant and perfect. Soft and strong all at the same time. I wanted to stay in a bubble in his apartment where he painted, and we did *it* over and over again. But his girlfriend, Jessica, would bring back reality with her perfect little bottom and Chinese food." I take a deep breath. "Okay, let's play now. The guy in the corner, buzz cut in the collared shirt."

"Just finished a stint in the army. He attends university to finish his math degree and become a high school teacher. See how he keeps glancing at his phone every few seconds? He checks the time waiting for his online date to show. She is a blonde hottie after an older man who took one glance at him and bailed because he looked cuter in the army uniform picture on Match."

Chapter Seven

Jennifer

I itch and squirm in my seat as I drive up the mountain. "This girl is on fire" blares on the radio, and I smirk at the irony. I can't sit still and keep hitting the gas harder than I should so I can get there and scratch my muff-less muff without the five teens in my loser cruiser noticing my bizarre behavior.

A Brazilian wax is overrated. No one thought to tell me I'd turn into a plucked chicken with poison ivy. The cream helps, but I can't apply it and drive at the same time. My tortured beaver screams in agony.

"Mom, turn this song up." The kids sing at the top of their lungs to the ear-splitting pop music. They continued the entire three-hour drive, killing any sanity left.

When I finally pull into the gravel drive, two moms and three new Crew dads greet me. All sit on the front steps of the cabin gazing at their shoes. Men? There are men at the cabin this weekend? Holy shit taco, this is new.

We spend the weekend in the woods for an Adventure Crew outing twice a year. Our troop rents several cabins for twenty-five teens and their leaders to mingle with other troops throughout the state. The kids love it, and I live for the hikes in the woods. Leaving two of my kids with Jake to fend for themselves at home is good for us. It reminds them of the various chores I do, mainly cleaning and making meals three times a day.

In the past, a gaggle of moms spent the weekend talking and laughing at their teens with never enough sleep for anyone. With men in attendance, the dynamics will change. Shit, men. I only brought sweatpants and my favorite scarf.

"Ugh, there goes number one and two on my checklist," I mumble before getting out of the teen hauler.

"What did you say, Mom?" My kid leans over me and grab the snacks off the front seat.

"Nothing, just thinking out loud." I take the keys out of the ignition and open the door.

Teens stream out of the cabin with cheerful shouts and whooping noises. "You're here. Finally."

"Hey. We're so happy to see you. We need serious reinforcement," one of the cranky moms says. "It's crisis mode in the cabin. A trashed mess. Mold covers everything. We can't sleep in the beds, and the fridge is engulfed in green…well, fuzzy green spores."

Sarah, a fellow PTA mom, walks to the back of my family mobile to check inside. "We need help. We got most of the upstairs clean but ran out of disinfectant supplies."

One of the burly guys says, "Any chance you brought some cleaning products with you? We are desperate."

I pass the cooler to him with my mouth wide open and my beaver still itching like crazy. This isn't any old dad, but a superhot one with a six-pack or maybe even an eight-pack under those clothes. His T-shirt stretches across his chest tight, exposing biceps I can't comprehend. He smiles and stares at me waiting for a response. Can I scratch or will he notice? I push my legs together instead and dance a little to reach the itch.

"So did you?" he asks.

"Did I what?" I ask and uncurl my scarf. Shit, did he want something?

"Did you happen to bring cleaning supplies up here with you?" He glares like I might be unstable.

"I did," I stammer, wiping the drool from my mouth with the back of my hand. "I always stock a few containers of Clorox wipes in the van. It's in the trunk." My face flushes red, and I yell across the yard, "Kids, touch nothing. It's gross inside."

Hot dad looks down at my dancing legs and says, "Oh, you can go to the bathroom first. It's okay. We'll unload for you."

I die right there when a chorus of surly preteens yell, "Mom."

"Our hero," yells another male voice sounding like our friend Dean from home. I turn and find him behind me holding the huge six-pack of wipes. He adjusts his black-rimmed glasses.

"Hi, Dean." He hugs me tighter than usual, and my breasts smush into his hard chest. He must work out now.

"Hi, Jennifer. Happy you're here this weekend. Where is your blockhead husband?" he whispers in my ear so no one else can hear.

"Yeah, right. You know he doesn't support extra activities with the kids."

"I know. He sucks." His sympathetic face hits me

in the gut. Dean never holds back his distaste for Jake. It started years ago when Jake signed up to be an assistant soccer coach, but of course, he didn't show up for practice or games. I stepped in and filled the volunteer role with sexy, computer geek Dean. Our friendship formed by commiserating over our lousy spouses.

Dean, an active dad who loves spending time with his kids, has full custody of his brood since his brutal divorce. His ex-wife wanted only a few weekends a month. After stewing for months, Dean reinvented himself. A stylish wardrobe and new haircut caught the attention of every school mom. I check out his tight jeans and collared shirt. Blood pounds through my body.

"Hero? It must be DEFCON five in there." I grin at the Hulk dude carrying a load from my car to the cabin. "Point me in the direction to clean. Well, once I deal with this Brazilian muff itch." I wiggle my legs again to ease the pain.

Hulk dad barks out a laugh. "Oh, this weekend will be interesting. You're a whippersnapper."

Holy shit taco, I realize too late I said the Brazilian part out loud. My sugar cookie has finally taken over my brain.

****

"Mom, Mom, Mom, can you hear me? There might be a fire in the kitchen. Maybe. Sorta." Half asleep, my kid yells in my face. I lift my head from the pillow and open one eye.

"Something might be on fire? Wait. What?" I turn over and look at the clock, six a.m. I roll back and stare at Kevin with brain fog. Oh yeah, we are at a cabin in the woods with the Adventure Crew. I hum with the memory of yummy Dean who kept his smile on me at dinner last night. My eyes drop closed. What I need is sleep and a dirty dream about Dean.

"Mom, do you hear me?"

Shit, I smell smoke, and a fire alarm blares.

"Uh, Dad, we need help right now," another kid yells from downstairs.

"What's happening?" I jump out of bed and run out of my room with a sweatshirt in hand to throw over my tank top and panties.

Dean stands at the top of the stairs. "It's okay, all under control." He places his hand on my arm. "It wasn't a real fire. The teenagers destroyed the toaster oven."

I sigh in relief.

"Looks like you need a little more sleep?" He scans my messy bun hair and peruses down my body.

"Yeah, yeah, fear of fire won out over need for sleep."

"Well, you look good, Jennifer. You always do. The crazy bun adds character."

I want to run my fingers over his freshly shaved face, his tight jeans, or his worn flannel shirt. I can't help myself. I lick my lips as he stares at my breasts. My hard nipples greet him. My neck warms, and I pull my sweatshirt over my head.

"Ha, thanks, Deeeaaaannn," I draw out his name in a smirky manner, and he grins back. "I need a seriously strong cup of coffee to get going. False alarms and morning screams aren't my usual wake-up call." I hide my unbrushed morning breath with my hand.

"I get it. I thought the teens might sleep in since

they stayed up so late. I hoped for a few quiet moments with a cup of coffee myself." He steps closer and blocks me from going down the stairs. The scent of cedar and citrus lingers between us. His body heat warms my skin. "You normally a morning person?" Why does he want a conversation while I am a bedhead mess?

"Not much. Not until after I drink my first cup of caffeine." I find myself inspecting his package. Looks good in those jeans. I blush and meet his eyes. He lifts his brows.

I am some sex-crazed, doddering woman. "We should…" I motion down the stairs and accidentally hit his hard, flat stomach. A mere inch separates us.

"Tom is down there, so it isn't as urgent as it sounds," he whispers in my ear with a grin. "But we should get a beautiful woman like you some coffee so you can function properly." He runs his fingers through my hair and goes down the stairs. I stand rooted in space and ogle his fine ass.

"Get yourself ready for the day. I'll bring it up to you. Then, you'll owe me later," he says over his shoulder.

The thought of owing Dean inspires me during my shower.

****

Dean and I lean on the porch rail as we watch the troop leave disappearing into the thick woods. All-day, we volunteered for the same chores or activities. After taking the kids out on the lake for the afternoon and pulling five kayaks from the rental facility, we took a "break" and offered our services for kitchen duty.

I peek at him. He gives me the same ravishing stare

he gave on the lake and the five-mile hike this morning. I smile back and bat my eyes. Even dressed in my gray sweats, I flirt back, making it clear I am interested.

"So alone adult time. I didn't see it on the schedule, but we should take it," Dean says.

"I could use a little free time." I throw my scarf on the railing. "The kids are great, but the constant noise and talking stresses me."

"Remember the Texas soccer tournament a few years ago, it lasted for two days? You kept hoping for a loss so we could go home. I, on the other hand, wanted to stay all week. But then, I only had two kids in my car. You had six or seven? Right?"

"Oh, the weekend from hell? I remember it well. Cold, rain, and I had six kids to chaperone by myself. Jake never attends all-weekend events for the kids. It's too much work. The other team parents bailed at the last minute, too. Plus, one of the kids had a mild cold. It was terrible, no adult free time then."

"Let's take it now," Dean murmurs in my ear and leans closer.

I grab my scarf and walk inside to the kitchen expecting him to follow. When I turn, he's gone. "Shit," I say in the quiet, messy room. Where did he disappear? I hoped for something naughty to happen. Adult free time sounded like adult sexy time. A man like Dean is too good for me. Maybe he doesn't find the sweats seductive enough. "Ha," I say out loud, walk into the living room, and throw myself on the sofa. Loser me. I'll take a much-needed nap instead.

Miles Davis' "Kind of Blue" comes soaring from upstairs. Hmm, what's this about? I investigate and find Dean upstairs in his room lying on the king-sized bed reading a book. His opened flannel shirt exposes his muscular chest.

"Um, I don't mean to disturb you." I step into the room.

"No, you can't disturb me. Please come in. I need some downtime, especially with you." Dean pats the space next to him.

My head swims. "Okay." I sit on the side of the bed. How am I in another man's bedroom? Next thing I know, I snuggle up to him while he presses his thumbs into my back and strokes up my stiff neck. I let out a faint moan. "It feels amazing. Don't ever stop." I am committed now. My husband hasn't massaged any body part in a long time.

Dean takes his time on my shoulders, and my muscles release tension from the day, from my life. I close my eyes and lean closer into his body. It smells of cedar and man. "Mmm…" I moan.

He bends down and nips my neck with his mouth. Another man kisses me. Have I lost my mind? And with Dean? Wet kisses line my skin. I force myself to stop worrying and hum again a little louder this time. Slowly, he kisses down to my shoulder with a gentle touch. My body relaxes into each kiss, and my panties get wet. "This okay?" he whispers with his tongue in my ear.

"Yes."

After a positive sign from me, he pulls me off the bed. His warm minty breath covers my body. His tongue swirls lower down my neck while he pulls off my sweatshirt. "Yes," I confirm again.

Shit, this experiment is worthy. Thank you, Anna. I'm in my head again thinking about the sex writing project instead of Dean. What is wrong with me? I shake my head a little to get back into the moment. Relax and observe every single detail to write later.

"You are so soft." Dean pulls me closer to his mouth and exposes my new purple push-up bra. He unsnaps the clasp and tugs it off my shoulders then trails kisses around my breasts giving each one ample attention. He licks around the tips of each peaked nipple.

The arousal shocks me. I'm wet, more than ever, and still completely dressed. I take steamy notes in my head, as my body responds to his movements. He is good at this. I don't want to forget a single thing.

I unbutton Dean's pants and kneel as I pull them off. Commando, his cock jolts out ready to play and is huge compared to Jake's. I take him in my mouth and show how much I appreciate him.

Dean stammers something I can't hear. I stay kneeling and plunge him farther into my mouth. Jerking, he says something again, and I listen this time.

"You don't need to do this. I like…" he moans, "Oh Jennifer, we need…"

I grin. I made him speechless. His face flushes with desire, and it makes me crazy hot. I might climax from his deep guttural noises.

"Wait. I don't want to… I…ohhhhh, yes… No wait. I want to see you first."

He drags me up his warm body. I kiss his mouth, and my tongue strokes against his. He rips off my hideous gray sweatpants.

"I hated these sweats but look how easy they slide off. And these." He gestures to my matching purple lace bikinis. "What you hide underneath is perfect.

Jennifer, you are so fucking beautiful."

I smile at my new naughty lingerie. In my early twenties, before mom clothes, I wore lovely push up bras and matching panties. With babies came saggy elastic maternity panties. Jake didn't care what I wore, so I bought sensible pieces after the baby weight fell off. This new writing project inspired me to wear beautiful lingerie again. Knowing something sexy is underneath the mom uniform makes me a warrior woman.

"Fuck, Jennifer, I am hard as a rock for you." Dean shows his approval.

Instead of sliding off the bikinis, he licks his way down my stomach to my now throbbing center. The wet fabric and his tongue make my knees buckle. Dean catches me and eases me onto his bed.

"I want to hear you, Jennifer. Make lots of noise for me. Remember, we can't be heard in the middle of the woods. No one will return for hours. The house is ours, and I plan to use my time wisely." He fumbles with a condom wrapper, but I don't open my eyes.

With my panties still on, his tongue slides up and down until I can't take another minute of this torture. He pushes them aside forcing me to call out for more. My body squirms from the intense sensations. My lady parts will never be the same. I scream for him, "Oh fuck, Dean. You are a yogi master with your tongue." After what felt like sexual punishment, he tugs the panties off.

Dean scans me splayed out on the bed panting for more and chuckles. He plunges into my buzzing wetness. Heat overwhelms me as he delves deep inside. My mind floats as if high on some drug, and I go off again in seconds as he plows into me with an urgency and passion I forgot existed. Oh, and he hears me loud and clear the whole time.

Chapter Eight

Jennifer

Searching for a calm place, I wander onto the cabin's front porch and inhale the fresh scent of pine. Teens continue to scream in the background. I pull out my phone to call Jake. The phone rings, and I wait for the latent guilt to set in, but it never does. After a dozen rings, he picks up and passes the phone directly to the kids without saying hello.

"Huh, guess Dad didn't want to say anything," I tell my daughter.

"Yeah, he's busy," she replies.

"Really? What did he plan for tonight?" I tug at the scarf wrapped too tight around my neck.

"Mom, come on. You know the game's on TV. He ordered pizza and told us not to bother him."

"Right," I respond, keeping myself from saying anything ugly. Sure, he is home with the younger kids, but he can't even be bothered to do something special with them.

"Well, get to bed at a decent time, sweetie."

"I will, Mom."

"I love you."

"Love you, too." She hangs up, and I take a moment to myself.

I smile and bask in the excitement from the tryst

with Dean. My panties dampen thinking of the secret looks he sent my way. At dinner, he sat next to me and played with my legs under the table. It made my nipples hard and ready to go again.

Keeping my eyes on the kids, I hoped no one noticed a change between the two of us. After eating mac 'n' cheese and salad, I offered to wash the dishes, and he cleared the table. He pinched my butt on the way into the kitchen and whispered, "Game on after the kids go to bed."

I can't wait. No sleep for me tonight. This is too much fun.

After midnight, I sit up in bed. Crickets chirp in the distance, and the kid chatter finally settles down for the night. My phone dings. I look down and a text from Dean greets me. A grin spreads across my face. I'd given up on anything happening tonight.

—You ready?—

My keys click as I quickly hit him back.

—Ready for what?—

—Take off your panties and meet me outside behind the cabin.—

—I thought you liked my lace?—

—I like what is underneath a lot more.—

I slide the black lace down my legs, pull on the one skirt in my luggage, and push my feet into sandals. Dean won't work hard to get me off. I am ready to play. For a moment, I consider standing in the window and touching myself for him, but I don't want to delay the fun. Plus, what if a kid saw me. Talk about a seriously disturbing situation.

I squint in the darkness. A cool breeze causes goose bumps to line my skin. Without a full moon or lights, I catwalk like Ingrid Bergman from *Casablanca*.

I don't know which direction he will arrive from, and a shiver runs down my spine. I stand there for a brief moment letting the excitement build. A stick snaps on the ground, and I freeze. He reaches around my waist, pulls up my skirt, and pushes himself against me from behind, hard already. "Oh," I moan. "Yeah, I want you in me again right now. Please, Mr. Handsome Lumberjack," I tease.

"You know it's me. No one else wants you as much as me, do they?" His voice catches as if this might be a real question.

"Only you and your fine body." I lean further into Dean's chest.

He wastes no time sliding his hand under my shirt onto my breasts and kissing my neck with a wet tongue. I still can't see him, and he doesn't say another word. His warm, spearmint breath tingles up and down my neck, moving and swirling his tongue. I love this game, strangers meeting in the night, an accidental coupling.

"I want it rough and hard this time," I whisper. "I can't scream, but force it out of me anyway. I want all of you in me."

Dean groans in my ear as he pushes his hand farther up my shirt, squeezing my breast hard. He sends me spiraling. He turns me around and holds me flush against his hardness. His hands fondle my breasts, and his breath tickles my neck. I push his sweatpants down and touch him bare in my hands.

"Damn, no condom. I forgot and left it in the room upstairs. Sorry."

"I fucking want you in me right now. I can't get pregnant, and I am clean. You?"

"Clean," he responds and plunges into me with a deep sigh.

Filling me completely, like I ask him too, he rocks his hips. This time, he grabs and moves hard instead of the slow exploration from before. Without the condom between us, the strong sensation pulses. This is everything.

Dean explodes in me and slides out. His absence creates a loss like a missing limb. I take a moment to wonder about the feeling as it is new. We connect perfectly. After a few minutes in the quiet of the forest, he pulls out and away from me. "Pure bliss," he whispers.

"Mmmhmmmmm," I growl.

"Goodnight, beautiful." He kisses my cheek and sneaks back inside the house.

I want to chase him to get more, thrust him inside of me again, pushing and prodding one more time for the night. Instead of running after him like a maniac, I count to twenty and creep back inside. I trip over a flip flop in the doorway and giggle softly at my lame effort to stay silent. I won't be able to sleep, so I'll take research notes for our sex book. Holy taco, this is fun. I can't wait to turn in pages to Anna.

****

Anna and I sit in a pink fabric-covered booth, and I take a bite of my muffin. A speck of powdered sugar falls on the crumple of papers in front of me. I brush it off with a napkin. "Well?" Anna sets my folder onto the table and beams with pride. Okay. I interpret her smile as pride because I finally did this shit.

"Yeah, this is a million times better. I'm not sure what to talk about, the writing or you doing *it* with

Crew dad Dean."

"Fucking amazeballs. I need to edit the manuscript, but I couldn't wait to show you the rough draft. I want you to know that I did my part in this experiment, too. Anna, the sex though. Dean makes me…"

Anna's head snaps up. "Whatever. Jennifer, you cannot get attached to a man. It was just for our project. No emotions. You know this."

"Yeah, of course. I know, but Dean's body amazed me. I tell you, Anna, he knows what to do with his dick. I can't believe his wife left him, such an idiot. I had no idea any man could perform such acts. Maybe there's something to an older, experienced guy."

"He isn't older than you." Anna smirks and laughs.

"I know. Right. Going into middle-age might bring some perks. Holy taco, men might finally get it."

We giggle like teenagers and keep reading and talking until the waiter informs us the coffee shop will close in thirty minutes.

I sigh. This new coffee shop on the other side of town sucks. Anna feels safer coming all the way over here, and I understand. She gets a refill of hot water for her tea, and I set my folder into the writing pouch of my messenger bag.

"Let's play," she says and sits back down.

"Yeah, her?" I point to a much older lady two tables away from us.

"Interesting choice." Anna glances around at the full tables. "Apparently, we aren't the only ones shocked by a nine p.m. closing on a Friday night."

"No shit. Okay, your turn," I say nodding again at the gray-haired woman.

"She is former FBI. She moved to our sleepy town

when she retired, mainly to hide out. She made enemies throughout the world and currently a mass murderer hunts her down. She knows, but the idea of him searching stimulates her. She wants to catch one more serial killer before she dies and lock him away forever. It's the only thing left on her bucket list. In her spare time, she reads to the blind and hula dances."

I spit out a little coffee on my scarf when she says hula. "Feeling dark tonight, huh?"

"A bit."

"Anything you want to talk about?" My eyebrows knit together.

"No. Really, I'm okay. Just a little down today. Nothing specific." She sips her tea. "I love this jasmine green. Remind me to order it next time."

I smile at my sweet friend. "Like I will remember?" We both laugh and gather our purses. "Oh, any more special body part texts?"

"They keep coming. I change my password every other day now and never check my phone in front of the kids or Luke."

"Why don't you block him? Is it worth the stress? Anna, I worry about you."

"Yeah, I kinda like getting them."

"I get it." I push the door open to leave. "I totally do."

****

Anna

"Stop shouting in a public place," I say through gritted teeth to my kids. I lean toward Jennifer and whisper, "I'm so tired." After my adventure with the baristo, coming to our family hang out place creates weird tingles down my spine, but there is no way I can keep the kids away from the pinwheels.

"Long weekends suck." Jennifer lets out a puff of air. The kids battle with their cookies, and we pretend to enjoy our time with them. I love them dearly, but I'm tired. She catches my eye and leans toward me. "You can't keep your eyes off him."

"I know." Heck, I know. Damn, he's brilliant. And even as Jennifer confronts me with it, my eyes gaze at his body. His tattooed arms press down at the espresso machine, and I picture his naked bottom.

"Ahh, shit, you don't have a crush, do you?" Her eyebrows arch. I blush and avert my eyes. "You do?"

"No, but he's gorgeous." I bury my face in my hands. What will I do?

"I don't think you're the only one." Jennifer directs her eyes to another table.

"What do you mean?"

"Look over there." She points with her hand still on her cappuccino to a couple of young twenty-somethings.

The perky-breasted, feathered hairdos giggle, gawk at him, and whisper to themselves. He glances over at them and smiles. They all but faint. I cross my arms. Why did she point them out?

"And there." Now, her little finger points to the corner at a thirty-something, nursing a coffee. The brunette woman ogles him like he's the only channel in the world and bats her eyes. The way she drinks her latte with her lips pursed all sexy turns my stomach. He winks at her, and she glows back. "Looks like he's got one for every decade. Twenties, thirties, and you're the forties."

My heart sinks. I glare at Jennifer. I'm not in the mood for teasing. She doesn't notice or doesn't care. The kids' eyes glaze over their tablets. "Whatever."

"Do you think he fucked both of the twenty-year-olds together, like at the same time?" she whispers in my ear and smirks as if picturing it.

"Heck, probably." I clench my teeth together.

"What did you say?" my seven-year-old asks.

"Time to go." I need to get out of here. "Storytime at the library is about to start."

We pack up the whining kids and drag them out to Jennifer's teen chariot through protests insisting they didn't get enough cookies or some other nonsense.

As I push the door open, he calls out, "Anna." I turn my head and his smile greets me. His eyes meet mine, and he passes me an iced mocha I didn't order. I reach to take it, and his hand grazes mine. He leans in. "I finished the painting. Come see it anytime."

My face turns red, and I nod yes. Jennifer can't suppress her laughter. But I'm struck by his flirty smile. Damn, it nearly knocks me out.

****

Jennifer

To kill my writer's block, I go to my favorite bakery and coffee shop during my scheduled writing time. I bowed out of a school PTA meeting to make more time in my planner. I don't normally eat sweets, but they sell the best French press coffee, muffins, and I love their deep, comfortable sofas.

I plan to get some decent chapters written or something valid and sexy for Anna to read. She won't find my one conquest, Dean, interesting compared to all her sexy action. “Super large black coffee and a blueberry muffin please.” Exhausted, I order the largest cup of coffee ever sold.

My gaze darts around for handsome men in the shop. I don’t find a single one and contemplate how I will meet my next sexy time victim, my new name for our book characters.

“Uh excuse me, ma’am.” The cash register guy glares at me. “I asked if you want room for cream. Twice.”

“No. Just black,” I snip back. He rolls his eyes and passes me my giant muffin.

“Thank you,” I say, checking him out. Too young for me to mess with, but not ugly.

“I guess you are welcome then.” His gaze slides up and down my body, letting me know he saw me gawking. Busted, I blush.

After picking a table, I jerk the man list from my wallet. The small tightly folded paper wears at the creases. I review the different types of men I want to screw, and my neck warms. Anna wants another chapter by tomorrow. Fuck, no ideas come to mind for where to meet a man, and I need something to write.

I take out my laptop and Google search for local bars open at nine a.m., but I get lost in the internet maze. An hour later, I find myself on some trite blog site about skincare and fashion when I notice a man in a tailored blue suit two tables over. His athletic build wears the suit well. Soft, curly hair flops into his eyes, and I want to touch his light-brown skin. I give him a long stare and return to my computer screen. He’s way out of my league.

He clears his throat and says, “Excuse me, but do I

know you? You look so familiar, but I can't place your face."

"Uhh," I stammer and peer around the room. Is he talking to me? Holy taco, did he see me checking him out?

He examines me with intention now. "Maybe it's work? Maybe you live near me? Do you run?" He pushes his thick hair out of his eyes and cocks his head to the side as if to say, well?

I flush bright red and fiddle with my red scarf. His smug grin looks like he's caught me at something naughty. This man is underwear model beautiful. My face reaches the deep shade of holy shit pink, and I blurt out, "Sorry. I don't think so…I don't run, uh, unless being chased. I'm sure I'd remember you."

"I swear we know one another. Are you a lawyer by any chance?"

"Definitely not."

"Okay." He smiles. "So you haven't sued me? Do you work downtown?"

"Not for many years." I shake my head. Did I put makeup on this morning? Geez, did I even brush my teeth?

"Wait. Do you have a son that plays soccer?"

I grin. "You caught me. I'm on the field constantly."

"Yes. Of course, I coach down there. I guess that is why you look familiar, and I think I know you. Sorry to bother you." He lifts his laptop screen.

Say something smart and flirty. Hurry. Say something smart and flirty. I can't think of anything to get his attention. Instead of being clever, I ramble. Shit. "Uh, well…uh…soccer…yeah, huh." Words fail me.

He smirks and gives me a wink with his crystal blue eyes.

I freeze. He winked. Do men still wink? Is something in his eye or is he flirting? Does he feel bad for me? Holy taco, I sit and stare at him like an idiot. I think all is lost until he closes his laptop again.

I take a deep breath and glance around the empty coffee shop. The employees remain glued to their phones. Suit man walks over, bends down next to me, and puts his hand on my knee right at the tear in my jeans. He pushes his finger in the hole and wiggles it around. My body tingles. “Nice jeans.”

I smile and lick my lips, victim number two. Game on, Anna, I scream in my head.

“You should see what I wear underneath them.” Holy shit, I can’t believe my forward mouth.

His eyes widen, and he whispers, “There’s a private conference room in the back. You can show me.” He gestures with his head to the closed door in the back corner of the coffee shop.

I stand, grab my computer, and head toward the room. A quick glimpse over my shoulder reveals a shocked face. “Gonna come play?” I puff up my chest. I can’t believe I’m so bold. Before I step into the conference room, he’s behind me with his hand on my lower back.

“I always wanna play,” he whispers into my ear.

The back room holds one large conference table and no windows. I shiver from the freezing AC blowing down on us. I place my computer on the table. The smell of his manly cologne engulfs me. He pushes hard and long against my leg, and it makes me instantly hot. This guy doesn’t care about my middle-aged boobs or smile wrinkles. He wants me. I must get out of my head to go through with this game. I focus on his shoulders and place my arms around his neck. It works.

"Are you going to show me what's under those jeans now?" He grins, runs his hand down my side, and pulls me closer.

"Mmm." I turn around for a kiss, and he bends down to unbutton my now lucky jeans.

He falls to his knees before me and peels the jeans off with a sigh. "You are right. These scraps of lace are great, much better than the pants." He licks the outside of my red panties. "I bet you fuck like a rock star."

I stifle a giggle. Jake doesn't like to go down on me, so this is a new sensation. What's with these men who do it willingly and like it? Are they truthful? Pleasure spirals down my body. Who cares? My new waxing proves beneficial.

I explode with his mouth on me and moan too loud for a public place. He keeps swirling his tongue, and I don't even care that we are in the back room of a coffee shop anymore.

I'm triumphant. I throw my head back in ecstasy, enjoying the ride. I peak and glance up at a hipster woman with hot pink hair enjoying our performance. Her eyes widen, and she licks her lips. I mumble something to the guy on the linoleum floor and detach him from my crotch. She applauds. "What a show. What a great mother fuckin' show."

Chapter Nine

Anna

The phone rings and rings. "Pick up," I shout in my head.

"Hello."

"*Ciao*, Jennifer," I say. My voice shakes.

"Yes, who's this?"

"What do you mean, who's this? It's me, Anna."

"Anna? The number came up weird."

"Because I'm in Rome."

"What? I can't hear. The kids are too loud." She yells in the background, "Guys, be quiet. I'm on the phone." After a minute she's back. "What the fuck did you say?"

"I'm in Rome."

"Rome? What? Where?"

"You know Rome. The Coliseum, Roman Forman, Vatican City, the Pope. Rome. Rome, Italy."

"What did you say? I saw you yesterday. How the fuck are you in Rome?"

"No time to get into the details. My phone card won't last long. I just lost it. I told Luke I needed to leave for some writing weekend thing. For the first time in forever, he has to take care of the kids alone. I got on a plane, and here I am."

"Holy taco, in fucking Rome?"

"Yes, in Rome. You gotta speed this up. My phone card is half-finished."

"You're in Rome and you want me to speed up the conversation? Okay, why did you call?"

"Well, I don't know what to do now."

"Why'd you go there?"

"It was the last place I remember being happy." I pause. How did I end up here? "I need more experiences. You know, to do ah…*it* for the book."

"Ha, nice. I love it. Then go out there and find some Italian men."

"But how? I was twenty and sexy, exotic even the last time I was here. But now I'm old and fat. Damn it. Compared to the Italians, I'm very fat. And my clothing looks cheap, and I don't know, I look American." I twirl my hair and wait for her response.

"Anna, you're not twenty or thin and you will never look like an Italian. Who cares?"

"Thanks. Whatever. Glad I called you."

"Wait. It doesn't mean you're not sexy or cute. And I'm sure there's an Italian guy your age you can hook up with."

"But how?"

"What did you do when you lived there in your twenties?"

"I worked as an au pair and went to college. You know this already."

"No, I mean what did you do for fun? Not the working part."

"I don't know. I met up with friends at piazzas. I wore high heels with short skirts and scarves like you do now. I ate lots of pizza. Drank coffee. Sketched the historic architecture and practiced Italian."

"Okay, great. You're in Rome. Don't worry about hooking up with anyone or the book. Just enjoy yourself."

"I guess you're right." I sigh.

"Of course, I'm right. And when you come home…" She pauses. "Shit, you will come home?"

"In seven days. I booked a flight back in a week. I better go. My phone card's almost out of time."

"Well then, in seven days you'll tell me everything."

"Okay, and, Jennifer, download WhatsApp so we can still text each other."

"Okay. What's the time difference?"

"I think about eight hours."

"Please come home."

"I will, *ciao*."

****

Jennifer

"Rome. How the hell did she get to Rome?" I say to my empty kitchen buried in dinner ingredients. I crank the tomato stew to simmer on the island cooktop and set the radio to NPR. "Today at the Vatican…" The news report forces me to drift away from the kitchen. Anna flew to Rome alone, without kids, chores, dinner messes, or her workaholic husband.

I survey the countertop and tidy away what I don't need any longer. I flip through my planner to today's list. Laundry day, water the plants, buy a card for Kevin's teacher, and send out the PTA minutes. I glance up at the clock. Ugh, in three hours I pick the kids up from their after-school activities, and the laundry remains untouched. I fold Jake's saggy tighty-whities and wonder about the nasty brown stains. I fling it to the carpet. Fuck this, writing time begins now. Forget the household chores and laundry.

Housekeeping dominates me no more. If I continue this route of drudgery, I will be brain dead at fifty.

I wake my computer. Anna's new chapters set in Rome will be full of wine, architecture, and pasta. My fingers fly over the keyboard. It may not resemble Rome, but I possess a tantalizing tale to share. Holy shit taco, Anna might not come home. Her sex adventure could prove more interesting than the life she left behind. I shake off the thought. She wouldn't abandon her kids. My head drops to the table and I sigh.

An hour into my writing, I get a text from Adventure weekend Dean.

—Thinking of you. Are you free today?—

I hold my thumbs above the phone call button for a minute. I crave my own Italian escape in the form of Dean but spending more time with him could be dangerous.

He types again.

—Hello. Is it me you're looking for?—

I reply.

—No one here and are you singing Lionel Richie? How old are you?—

No rebuking him, he replies.

—Gotta love an old romantic song. Plus, you know it's funny.—

I look at my phone. How to respond? Our banter comes too easy.

—Hysterical.—

—I wanna be with you tonight. I need to touch you.—

Shit.

—Dean, we're just friends. Our fun was a one-time thing, no more playtime.—

I stare at my phone waiting for a response. After a few minutes of nothing, I know he understands. "Ugh." I drop my phone.

The kids will demand snacks the minute they get home. I abandon my writing to chop up carrots and make hummus. "Back to the job of being Mom," I tell my kitchen.

****

The garage door creaks open as I scrape the dinner plates into the compost and load the dishwasher, Jake walks in late. "Hey, honey, I'm home. I hope ya cooked something good. Ya can go ahead and set my place. I'll go change out of this monkey suit."

Eyebrows lift and I say, "Oh, I already made and cleaned up dinner an hour ago. You promised to come home at six. Remember?"

"I did?" Jake questions.

"I'm outta here in twenty minutes for book club. You can order pizza or eat leftovers from the fridge."

Jake glares with a question on his face. "No, I didn't remember. You're leaving tonight? How nice for ya."

I ignore his rude comment.

"I thought book club was on the first of every month?"

"Yes, normally, but tonight is a special occasion. I told you about it this morning. It's on the family calendar. We're celebrating Anna's birthday, so we added an extra meeting this month. I lie about the occasion knowing he won't remember Anna's real birthday or check our family calendar. He never does. "I can't miss Anna's special party."

"Oh, well then…" Jake tries to smooth the irritation in the room. He picks up his phone and dials Pizza Hut. I sneak upstairs to get dressed.

Once in my mom van, I head on the interstate out of town. The need to escape tugs at me, and I drive fast. I abandon my planner and list for today. I miss Anna, although she just left. She feels too far away.

****

Anna

I mutter the plan out loud, "New clothes, piazzas, sketch, pizza, and practice Italian." Well, no time like the present. I take a deep breath and address the clerk at the front desk of the hotel saying, "*Avete una mapa del città?*"

"*Sì, signora.*" He produces a cheap tourist map showing the major attractions. I spot my destination and fold the paper.

"*Conoscete un posto che ha…*" Damn, I don't know the word for art supplies. "*Artista*?" I motion with my hand drawing on imaginary paper.

"*Sì, c'è un posto qui vicino.*" He escorts me to the street, points down the block, and gives directions.

"*Grazie.*"

I start off on my second Italian adventure, twenty-years later. Several shops sell clothing along the cobblestone street. There's no chance I can find a short skirt that will fit or look right, but I manage to score a pair of beautiful black boots. The cut hits under the knee with butter-like leather. It goes well with my black pants.

I add a black sweater with a scooped collar and a colorful scarf I find off a street vendor. I even toss my worn brown knapsack purse in the trash and replace it with a knockoff Louis Vuitton handbag. My new outfit doesn't make me appear twenty, but my walk takes on a sexy saunter.

I smile big at an old lady passing by me. She wears heels, fishnet stockings, and carries a cloth grocery bag. Damn, I love Italians. They know how to live. Of course, she looks at me like I'm simple. I forgot, no smiling in the big city.

The scent of warm bread greets me as I round the corner. I spot a narrow little shop with a 3D paintbrush above the sign. I step in. The shop's counter wraps around the room with little space to stand. The walls show off various sizes of paintbrushes and art supplies, a no-touch and ask for what you want kind of place.

A young woman, who stepped out of 1980's London punk scene, with a nose ring, ten earrings in each ear, a tongue ring, and coal-black hair scoffs in my direction. I bite my lip and fiddle with my purse strap.

Damn, I forgot what to say. "*Mi scusi, voglio le cose per scrivere*." I search for the right word. "*No, per*." I motion with my hand drawing a picture in the air. She stares back with earbuds in her ears. Can she even hear what I said? "*Carta*," I ask.

She proceeds with a list of things I don't understand in rapid Italian. Whatever.

"*No lo so*." I shake my head. She huffs and goes to the back. I wait. Is she coming back? I need charcoal pencils and a sketch pad. I search for Italian art words on my phone.

The back door opens with a click, and I glance up

ready with the word "sketch pad." Not the punk girl but a man in his fifties with graying dark hair and olive skin stands before me. He smiles.

"*Buongiorno, Signorina.*" He calls me a young woman. Brilliant.

"*Buongiorno. Voglio…*"

"Are you American?"

"Yes. Is my Italian that bad?" I bite my lip as my face flushes red.

"No, it's as lovely as you."

Damn, I love Italians. In a few minutes, he packs my things in pretty brown paper sealed with a gold sticker.

"So are you here with friends? Family?"

"No, just me. Time for myself."

"Where are you from?"

"Tulsa, Oklahoma."

"And how does a girl from Tulsa, Oklahoma, know Italian?" His deep, rough voice sends a tingle down my spine.

"Well, I lived in Rome for a year as an *au pair* twenty years ago."

"So a homecoming of sorts."

"Yes."

"And left behind in Tulsa, Oklahoma?"

"Let's not wreck a lovely day with talk of work and family."

"Yes, I agree. You are free now. For how long?"

"Six more days, counting today." I twirl my hair.

"And what are you desiring to visit?"

"*Fontana delle Tartarughe.*"

"Ah, not the most touristy of places, but oh so lovely and not far from here. Shall I walk you?" With his deep voice, he can walk me anywhere. I gaze into his warm brown eyes and nod *sì.*

"*Orella, guardi il negozio per un momento*," he shouts to the back of the store. A grunt comes from the other room. He holds the door. "My niece, a winsome creature, so young and idealistic. She doesn't believe in monetary exchange, and yet is forced to work in my shop for pocket money while she studies in philosophy at University."

"She doesn't believe in money?"

"No, she believes in nothing at this age." He holds out his arm. I link in, and his body heat sweeps over me. "We should be free, living without the oppressive government and establishment creating war, racism, poverty, and sexism. Let man to his own conscience guide him in a free world, no? Something like that anyway. I was never a punk. She is a beautiful girl if you can look past the face metal. I keep her on to help my brother from worry."

"If only the youth were so principled everywhere in the world."

"Yes, I guess you're right. Better to believe in principles, however unrealistic, than nothing at all. It is a nice day with blue skies. Perfect weather to escape my little shop. Free time feeds the soul."

"Do you have a lot of business?" I bite my lip at my overly personal question.

"Not a lot of street business, but I produce a catalog and the universities place orders. I get much of my inventory purchased directly from manufacturers here and abroad. I can make them good prices."

Thank goodness he took it the way I intended. "How interesting."

"And you? You must tell me something of yourself."

I pause. "I work as a teacher, kindergarten."

"Ah, the little ones. Sweet, but tiring, no?"

"Yes."

"And children, do you have any?"

"A boy and a girl." A pain hits my stomach as guilt invades my body. What did I do?

"Me too, a boy and a girl. But they are almost grown like my niece. Though not as idealistic as her. My daughter studies law and my son civil engineering."

"Mine are young, still in elementary school." How can I change the subject? I don't want to talk about my family.

He probably senses my tension as he moves on to my passion. "So your artistic endeavors, tell me about them."

"Oh, I paint and draw, but not for a long while. I'm not any good, but I enjoy making things. It's time for me to get back to my art. I write, too."

"Very good. We need to take care of ourselves. Americans are too obsessed with work, work, work. What do you write?"

"I write novels, mostly romance."

"We may not be the city of love, but Rome sees plenty of romance." He stops at a stand and buys a yellow mimosa wrapped in cellophane. I noticed the stalls around the city earlier in the day. "*La Festa Della Donna*." He hands me a bunch of small yellow blooms. "You must receive flowers today."

"Oh yes, I remember. Women's day. They decorate the entire city."

We turn into the neighborhood leading to the

fountain. Clothing hangs from lines out windows and balconies. The intimate, narrow streets close in around us. He stops and smiles at me a moment.

"Well, your fountain is up this walkway. Please stop by the store after your visit with the turtles." He leans in to kiss each cheek, my left side first, but I turn my head right and our lips graze.

"Sorry." I bite my lip and touch the spot his lips brushed against mine.

"No, no, our silly Italian customs." He leans in again.

This time I don't move and receive a small peck on each cheek. I wish for more, but I smile and walk to the fountain alone. My heart sinks, and I shake my head to clear all thoughts of him. Whatever, just an Italian man giving me a little bit of attention.

I'm in my favorite place in Rome, no man needed. Even though nothing in Rome seems the same as my first visit, the fountain looks exactly the same as when Landini made it five hundred years prior.

Chapter Ten

Anna

The statuary of young men and turtles still holds intrigue. I sit on a cold stone bench and open my new art supplies. Not wanting to make a mess, I sharpen a pencil into my new handbag even though cigarette butts litter the cobblestone streets.

I turn to a fresh sheet of paper in the new sketchbook and draw. My mind focuses on the paper and the fountain. I pay attention to the small details in the turtles and the curved bodies of the men immortalized in bronze. Much later, someone calls my name.

Allessandro from the art shop stands before me. "It's already midday. You slipped away into your work. I thought you passed by the store without saying hello but decided to check. You desire lunch, no."

"*Ciao*, I lost track of time. Yes, lunch and something to drink. What time is it?" I bite my lip.

"Half-past one by now."

"Wow, I focused on my art for hours."

"Yes, I can tell. You have talent." He inspects the sketch. "Well, I'd suggest a coffee and refreshment, but nothing is open at this time in the afternoon."

"Of course, I forgot the afternoon *riposo*."

"But you must eat. Let's go to my small apartment

above the shop. It isn't grand, but the *Moka* pot works, and I can scrounge up something decent to nibble on. Then you can return to your fountain."

"Thank you. Sounds brilliant."

I stroll beside him through the quiet, cobblestone streets to his little shop. He unlocks the apartment door beside the metal garage gate covering of the store. A flight of stairs leads to his place.

The apartment opens into a room with tall ceilings and large windows. White sofas and armchairs sit on an antique tile floor. A thick, wood bookcase stuffed full of trinkets and books from exotic places catches my eye. A little kitchen stands on the other side of the room with a two-burner stove and a half fridge.

He rummages through his cupboards. I relax at a glass table over a Persian rug. "I love your place, so crisp and sunny. Do you travel a lot?"

"Define a lot?"

"How often do you leave town?"

"I make at least one trip a year for pleasure, but I tend to do more for work. I import specialty items."

"Of course. I didn't think about you going to the suppliers."

"Best way to do business. My wife hates the apartment, but a man and woman should keep their own places. This is mine. She doesn't even possess a key. Her opulence and style far exceed this space anyway."

"Wife?" My heart drops but why should it. I have a husband, but I intentionally did not mention him.

"Yes. We keep ourselves apart mostly but still spend a few nights together each week. After many years of marriage, she dislikes my company, and I feel the same. Though our arrangement works for us."

I twirl my hair. Is he saying we should just be friends because he's a married man or something else? I thought this was leading to…whatever.

"Italians and their complicated marriages. We stay together and yet make our own happiness, too." Ah, the stereotypical Italian with their lovers.

He puts together some red pasta with a lovely spread of cheeses, meats, and olives. I eat the savory food a little too heartily. Damn, I should be daintier.

"Let's take our wine on the couch." He slides in beside me and soft Italian music plays in the background. Our bodies touch. How many women sat in this spot before me and how many will after? Whatever. He combs his hands through my hair and gazes into my blue eyes. "*Che bella*."

Damn, his baritone voice is too much. His lips touch mine purposefully this time. Before I know it, his hand explores under my blouse, and his tongue delves into my mouth. Both move with expert precision. He tastes of espresso, and I moan as his tongue brushes against mine.

His hand squeezes my breasts over my corset. I inhale the scent of him. He isn't all muscle like the bouncer or a perfect specimen like the artist baristo but the embodiment of romance itself, mature and sexy. He whispers things in Italian I don't understand. The smooth language and Allessandro's deep voice send shivers down my spine.

His tongue travels to my ear, and he circles around the lobe before plunging in and out. My panties moisten as his fingers glide across my arms. He kisses down my neck and continues talking. I understand counting in Italian and the word beautiful. Certain his next move will be to unbutton my blouse, I ready myself, but he kisses my lips and stands-up instead.

"Naptime, my *bellissima*. Pasta and *vino* first, now we need rest. Will you lie with me?" My body shrinks into the sofa from his confidence, his sexiness, his voice. I nod *sì*. "Okay. One moment." He disappears behind one of the only doors in the apartment and comes back with a white fluffy robe and a silk nighty.

Damn this man is prepared. "You can change in the bathroom if you wish." I do, but don't put on the nighty. Instead, I keep on the stockings and corset I wore under my clothing. I exit the bathroom, and he calls to me, "Come in here."

I follow his voice to the bedroom which can only be described as the most luxurious room designed by a man. Large white pillows sit atop a huge bed with a white duvet. And he rests in the center with his bare chest dotted in black hair. Should I strip? No. What should I do? I take off my robe in a fast motion and half fall half trip into bed.

"Oh my, you are sexy, no."

He flips a switch to turn off the lights, and I lay beside him. I tremble like a virgin on her wedding day. He turns to me and kisses me so well my toes tingle. His taste of musk and coffee linger in my mouth. Spinning me on my side, his warm body snuggles mine. Naked and hard, his tool pokes against my bottom. His hands caress my waist, but nothing more.

I wait, unsure if I should move until the room fills with his soft breathing. He fell asleep. Whatever. My gaze darts around the dark room before closing. Between the soft duvet, his warm body, or the jet lag, sleep pulls me under, too.

In a half-dream, soft kisses caress my neck. My eyes peek open, and I startle. "It's okay, darling. Just me, Allessandro." I recognize his rough voice immediately.

He continues with his kisses before rolling me toward him. The caress at my breast wakes me fully. He moans, and his mouth meets mine. Our tongues twist against each other in a dance. He mounts me revealing a toned chest. I touch his chest hair and run my hands over his body. He slips my lace undies down my legs and slides on a condom, and plunges into me.

I groan from the pleasure he gives me. His tongue meets my sensitive area again, and he plays it like a maestro. I endure, barely able to stay in my own skin. He flips me over and begins again.

He vibrates inside, in and out again. His tongue mirrors the motion in my ear. I'm beyond immersed in his expert hands, body, and tongue. He stops again and turns me over to face him but doesn't climb on me the way I expect. His tongue frolics on my lady parts. Damn it. My body nearly explodes, but he doesn't let it happen. He stops.

"No. No. No," I plead.

Ignoring my desperation, he pulls me over and pushes himself inside me. His body rests perpendicular to mine. I enter the Kama Sutra. Damn. The angle brings more pleasure. It forces in deep, and then out, nearly removing his tool each time. I beg for mercy and scream for release.

In control, he teases me grinning. He exits my body and rubs me with his skilled hands. The pleasure mounts to a level that hurts. My whole body vibrates, wanting to come. He lies on his back and tugs me onto him. On top, I slide him inside me and savor the power of this alpha position. He smiles as he cups my breasts in his hands. I glide up and down while he rubs with his fingers.

I never felt this out of control before. Frenetic energy bolts through my body. I must take him, my way, now. Sweat glistens over my body as I work hard and fast. His explosive moans increase, and I know his climax builds, too. It releases.

My body shudders in a series of pleasurable spasms and a wave of heat undulates through me. I think of nothing else but my body's response. My breath stops short and I can't move, completely at his mercy.

Damn it, he desires more. He whips me over and lifts my legs straight against his chest. He sinks deep inside me. His co…*weapon* thrusts in and out. He played me this whole time, teasing and smiling at my discomfort. I goad him too, but he holds me with his forceful arms. I submit and examine his serious face. Satisfied, I want him to experience the pleasure too. He screams as he gushes inside me.

Collapsed against me, our wet bodies cling to the satin sheets. He leans over a side table, and fumbles for something, a cigarette of course. How damn cliché but Italian. The room fills with vapor. I cough. I like to smoke when drinking, but it irritates me any other time.

"Sorry, dear. An old, nasty habit." He fans it away from me, but it keeps drifting up my nose in the same way cats bother only those who are allergic. He stands and displays his thick muscular, nude body in all its glory including a black mole on one of his butt cheeks. Opening the glass door to the little balcony,

Allessandro walks naked outside to smoke with the condom still stuck on his tool.

I snuggle up in bed with the duvet around me. My mind floats without a care in the world. He comes back but leaves the door open. The city noises and sunlight drift into the dark room.

"I'll get coffee," he says.

I wait for the coffee, and my heart fills with guilt about the money I spent to get here, and Luke at home taking care of the kids. I inhale and sink into the comfy bed.

He returns with two espressos in little cups, still naked but sans condom. I sit up with the duvet at my neck. He passes me my drink and yanks the covers revealing my body.

"Better." We drink in bed together. "So, *bella*, tell me why you really came to Italy."

I breathe in roasted, Italian coffee. "I…I kinda ran away."

"Ran away from what?" He tugs my corset and kisses my nipple.

"My family, my life." Tears roll down my cheeks and my stomach clenches as my guilt returns.

"Oh, no. No tears." He kisses them away. "It's okay to run. Sometimes you need to go, no?"

"I guess. I don't know. Whatever. The whole thing started with my best friend. We wanted to write an erotic book."

"Ooh-la-la. Sounds fun."

"Yes. But I couldn't write anything hot. I exist in a state of misery. Work stinks. School keeps me too busy, and I'm not cut out for it. My colleagues seem to revel in special projects like making pilgrim hats, and I can't even remember to enter my grades on time.

At home, the kids challenge my rules and never give me a break. I love the kids of course, but I'm tired of always being the mom. And my husband, we loved each other once, but damn, we don't even talk anymore. He's never around."

"Americans don't treat themselves to anything. Always so busy. The children are the center of everything, and moms drive everyone around to a million activities. Hardly anyone hires a housekeeper. No vacations either, no wonder you're tired. It's good you take care of yourself. You should indulge more."

"Yes, but I did *it* with other men, not just you."

"Well, sometimes you need a little fun, no." He kisses around my nipple. "What makes you happy?"

"Writing, painting, and family does, too."

"Sex, no? Food?"

"Yes, I do like sex and food." I smile.

He unfastens the garter clasp and unravels my stocking. He kisses my thighs. "You need to screw every day, eat good food, and write or paint. Every single day." He kisses my lips. "Every day."

I repeat, "Every day."

"Yes, then you won't cry any more tears. Just happiness, no."

"I guess so." Is it so simple?

He removes the other garter and unlaces the corset.

"Leave it on. I look better with it."

"Nonsense."

"I'm too fat."

"*Ciccia.*" He shrugs his shoulders and frowns.

"What does *ciccia* mean?"

"Uh, chubby but sexy. Don't hide yourself.

Remember to screw, eat, write, and paint every day. Screw first, no?"

"Okay."

He surveys my naked body, slides another condom on, and does me again, but not before rubbing his tongue all over me. I'm a puddle at his mercy. I climax in a big moan and my built-up tension releases. With a loud groan, he orgasms and collapses on top of me. He stays inside and kisses my lips.

His shaft submits to non-combat size, but somehow our bodies stay pressed together. Head resting on my shoulder, he whispers about me in Italian talking of my kindness, beauty, and talent. We close our eyes and sleep again. This time, jet lag contributes nothing to my exhaustion.

I awake in a sweat puddle with him still on me. I stir.

He smiles and kisses me again. "Douche?" I give him a weird look. "Shower. I mean shower, yes."

Two huge rain shower heads await in a glass chamber built for two. Hot water coats us as we stand side-by-side. He foams up my body massaging my muscles, kissing my lips, neck, and nipples.

We exit the shower, and he holds up a heated towel. He rubs me down and kisses my cheeks. His talented tongue slips into a dance with mine. He wraps a towel around his wet body.

"I will get your clothing for you, and there is a hairdryer in the cabinet if you need it. Darling, what is your hotel's name?"

"Hotel *Monte Cerici*."

He returns with my clothing. I dress, dry, and brush my hair. My make-up is smeared all over my face. I clean up and wish I kept my makeup bag in my purse. When I exit the bathroom, I find him reading the newspaper on the couch with two cups of coffee in front of him. My luggage propped at the door.

"My stuff?"

"I called the hotel and got the bellman to bring it over. You'd rather stay here, yes?"

Like a kept woman, I nod *sì*. Only three more nights left in Rome, and I'd rather stay with him. I snuggle up next to him and sip the smooth, roasted coffee.

"Shall we go for a *passeggiata* and find some dinner out?"

"*Sì.*" I smile. Brilliant.

Chapter Eleven

Jennifer

"Outside," I say again for the tenth time and shut the sliding glass door to the backyard. "It's a beautiful day, and you should enjoy it." I continue talking but no one listens. School vacation days stress my nerves. I fill the sink with soapy, hot water and work on the breakfast dishes.

The running water and methodical scrubbing give me time to think. I need to reevaluate my recent boy toy choices. Getting emotionally involved with an old dad friend was a terrible idea. If I don't want to get busted, I should stick with complete strangers. It makes a better story anyway.

Drying my hands, I check my watch for the third time in an hour and consult the family calendar. The kids will be picked up for a playdate any minute. I booked a late morning appointment with AT&T. The repair person should arrive shortly.

A red mom Volvo pulls up outside and honks. The kids run through the kitchen yelling, "Bye, Mom," and continue out the door.

I follow behind carrying water and gratitude. Passing the Volvo mom the reusable bottles, I thank her for the free time and run inside. In the quiet house, I flip through my planner glad for the extra minutes and space to write. I start a load of laundry and the first draft of my next chapter while I wait.

****

The rumble of a vehicle pulling up to my house takes me from my writing. I stretch, look out the window from my desk, and inspect the man sitting at the wheel of the AT&T van. The time on my computer reads eleven a.m. I sneak to another window to get a better view. I pull the curtain back a crack as a tall man steps out of the white business van. Holy taco, what a beautiful hunk. I fist pump the air then look down at my mom jeans and sweater. “Shit.”

I run to my bedroom and quickly strip off my clothes. No one can seduce dressed like an old lady. I look over the backless, bright-green skimpy dress waiting for me on the bed. My wardrobe contingency plan for seduction depending on who arrived. I throw it on without a bra and take off my panties to make this easy for him.

Before he can knock twice, I fling the door open and smile. “You going to fix me up?” I ask with raised eyebrows, and blatantly check out his hard-muscled body bulging out of the button-down work shirt. The tight fabric clings to his skin, showing me his chest and rock-solid biceps. His fingers comb black hair out of his eyes, and a grin spreads across his face.

“Yes, ma’am. Here to fix your…” Distracted, his eyes catch my nipples poking out like light beams toward him. “…wiring. Someone placed a work order for static.”

Shit, this will be easier than I expected. “Follow me.” I shake my long hair out of its rubber band and look over my shoulder. AT&T sent me Mr. Buff and

Beautiful. I hope he keeps the white hard hat and work boots on while we fuck. “Uh, you wanna maybe visit my bedroom first?”

“Excuse me?” He stops short. “Is there trouble in there too? I thought it was just your box.”

“Oh, yeah, it is my box.” I giggle at my junior high comment. He stands in the hall with his eyes flicking from me to his clipboard. I lift my dress over my head and throw it at him. I figure he can leave now if he needs to go. He freezes like a statue. I say, “Come on, big boy. Let’s play.”

He shakes his head like a dog shaking off water from a bath. This is not the house call he expected. One second later, he unbuckles his belt and follows. In the bedroom, he pushes down his pants to reveal Santa Claus boxers.

“Well, howdy Santa,” I say and jump onto the bed.

He crawls on me and takes charge. With a dirty grin, his mouth attacks my breast sending waves of pleasure through my body. I notice his bright blue eyes.

“More clothes off. Now,” I demand. He moves to throw off the hat. “Wait. Kill the shirt and boxers but keep the hard hat and boots.”

He chuckles, pulls a condom from his wallet, magically rolls it on, and sinks into me without further ado. I’m already wet. “Holy taco, please, make it last a long time,” I groan and murmur.

We create a rhythm, thrusting and moaning together. Our hands glide over one another’s bodies. He works inside of me forever. Sweat trickles down my breasts. “Oh, baby. Yes. Yes,” he orgasms and yells.

I come right behind him and want more.

“May I?” I gesture toward him. “Will it come back

quickly?" I lean to grab it but draw backward, waiting for an answer.

"Baby, take it all." He lounges at the edge of the bed while I kneel praying in front of his ripped, glistening body.

I focus on my work as excitement tingles all over my skin. It is thicker than anything I have ever seen. This man exemplifies hedonistic specimens.

"Wait. You can't finish. I need you in me," I say and slip off.

"All right. Sounds good." He reaches into his wallet for another condom. "I aim to please."

"Thank fuck for AT&T's customer service."

I spread my legs to show my excitement. He leans in to kiss the inside of my thighs and trails upward. I nearly climax at these kisses. With his hard hat still on, his ripped body moves up mine until we merge together on the parquet floor. I touch myself. "Oh, I think that is my job, baby girl," he growls.

He flicks his finger in me until I orgasm with a shout. "Oh fuck, holy taco, it feels so good."

Next thing I know, he rides me again with his amazingness pulling in and out harder than before. Pleasure spirals down to my toes. This roller coaster should never end. To slow down, I flip him over and force him flat. "Let me take you for a bit first."

Knees bent, I press my breasts into his face, and he sucks my nipples while I pump up and down on top of him. He fills me, and my grip tightens. Watching me, he climaxes into me with a low moan, biting down on my nipples hard enough to make me go again. Spent, my legs shake, and I can't move.

He lies on the carpet for a few minutes before

saying, “I really need to check your residential gateway, or my manager will be after me.”

“Sorry, there isn’t anything wrong with it.” I giggle like a small girl.

“You planned this?” He chuckles.

“No. Well, I left possibilities open. I wasn’t sure who would show up exactly. Think of it as a friendly hello. Plus, who doesn’t want to fuck the AT&T guy?”

“Well, hello then. Should I call you later?”

“No, definitely not. Never. My husband’s uptight. This was just one time, okay? Cliché sex checklist and a little Tuesday morning fun.”

“All right then. Certainly will be my favorite service call today. Thank you.” He puts on his pants, kisses my forehead, and the front door shuts behind him.

Chapter Twelve

Anna

The light streams in from a crack in the curtain and hits my face. I perk up at the scent of coffee. My hand reaches beside me and finds only empty sheets. I sit up and yawn as Allessandro walks in with a wooden tray.

"*Bella*, you are awake?" He places the tray on my lap with a smile and joins me in bed with a newspaper. I offer you a cappuccino, a peach, and a rose.

"Brilliant. You shouldn't have."

"For you, of course, I should, no?" He kisses my neck. "My darling, what do you want to do today? Visit your turtle fountain again?"

"No. Can we walk in my old neighborhood?"

"Where, my beautiful?"

"*Piazza Vittorio Emanuele II.*"

"Yes, with the nice market, no."

"And we could walk to the Coliseum from there."

"A walking tour, yes."

"First a bath, no?" He gets up and goes to the bathroom.

I take my last sip of cappuccino and follow him. The bathtub fills with hot water and bubbles. The scent of lilies overtakes the room. My nighty slips off as kisses cover my lips. I step into the water, and he kneels beside me to rub my shoulders. He takes a bath brush and scrubs my back, legs, and feet. With the detachable showerhead, he sprays down my hair and shampoos it. Allessandro's deep, relaxing massage rivals top salons. He rinses soap from my hair.

A wet mouth circles my nipples with kisses, and he moves the sprayer down my stomach and between my legs. I moan from the intensity, and he silences me with his mouth. The water pressure undulates back and forth in a slow rhythm matching our tongues. My apex burns with pleasure, and I move my hips to stretch out the experience. It doesn't. It builds up and releases in a flash. I moan, and he smiles. I move to get out of the bath and grab at his pants, wanting to return the favor.

He shakes his head no and says, "Later, relax now." He leaves me in the bathroom with my bubbles and lilies.

I doze off and jump when he returns. "Your water feels tepid."

"Yes." I shiver. He holds out a warm towel and starts drying. His kisses follow at my nipples and neck. Luke used to pamper me. Maybe not like this, but he did bring flowers and give massages. What happened to the romance? I used to meet him at his office occasionally to fool around or bring his favorite lunch. We were different people in a different time.

Allessandro wraps me up in the towel and holds out another one for my hair. I flip my head over and put the towel up into a turban.

"Come," he says.

I assume we will head to his bed, but I'm wrong. A massage table waits for me in the living room, and he motions for me to lie down. I do, and he places a hot towel on my back. Squirting lotion into his hands, he rubs them together to warm the cream. He pulls down the towel and massages my back.

"Where did you learn this?"

"Oh, here and there." He massages my entire body, every inch. All thoughts disappear as I sink into the table. Allessandro leans in and kisses me. "Well, my darling, we should get going."

I dress in the bathroom and come out in the same clothing I wore yesterday. "Sorry I didn't bring anything new to wear. The clothing I brought isn't very suitable."

"I picked this up for you. New scarf, a new outfit, no? The blue will pick up your eyes." It's as if I designed a man in a computer and Allessandro popped out.

"Brilliant. You're perfect."

"Aged to perfection, no?" He winks. His rough, sexy voice puts it over the top. I want to do him again. He opens the door and takes my arm. The long morning of relaxation pushed us past the afternoon *riposo*. We take a taxi to the *piazza*, and it's exactly like I remember.

The open-air market covers the square with stalls of fruits and veggies. We buy blood oranges and smoked mozzarella cheese in the shape of little pigs. I squeal with delight when I recognize the things from long ago. The international food store appears on the corner, and I want to go inside. Allessandro reminds me I'll be home tomorrow and to buy groceries is wasteful.

"I used to buy peanut butter there."

"Peanut butter. *Che schifo.* Americans eat odd food, no?"

"I love peanut butter."

"You are welcome to buy some."

"No. Whatever, plenty at home."

"Okay, you lead the way."

The *pizzeria* I frequented closed, but he assures me there are many others. We will eat at one of them tonight instead. We find the bakery I loved, and I insist on him letting me ask for bread by myself like I did for the family I worked for years ago.

"What will we do with all this food?"

"Eat it." And we do. We nibble on it little by little, making our lunch a walking one as we tour. We also find the cookie factory and load up on the pretty little things. I ask a stranger to take a photo of us together in front of the water fountain next to my old apartment.

"You know there are many of these all over the city, no?"

"Yes, but I love this one."

I make him take another photo of me plugging the hole of a running spigot. It forces water up through another spout so you can drink from it directly, making a street water fountain.

"Most tourists are interested in the Vatican and the Roman Forum, yes. But you…"

"I know, but I love the cobblestones and the fountains and the bread and the pizza and the little cookies tasting of vanilla." He smiles at my glee.

I shriek again when we wander into the park on the hill overlooking the Coliseum. "Oh, it's just the same."

"They really don't change the ruins, my dear."

"Whatever." I smile and twirl my hair.

Children play in the walkways and young couples sit on benches necking. We find our own bench and gaze at the traffic circle buzzing with activity around the Coliseum. We kiss like a young couple in love.

"It's almost sunset. Do you think he's still there?"

"Who?"

I don't respond. "Let's go." I drag him down the hill and across the busy street to the back of the Coliseum. "He is. Look." I point toward an old man with a pushcart setting out tins of food for the cats. Hundreds of cats come out of the monument toward him meowing. "Isn't it brilliant? Who thought he'd still be here all these years later? Do you think it's the same old man? Or are there more? Is it a club or individual initiative to feed the cats?"

"I don't know, my darling." The sun sets and the air fills with the happy cat meows. He grabs me and kisses my lips forcing our bodies together. "Now what, my darling?" He stares at me in his arms.

"We will eat pizza, vino, and gelato. Then, we visit the *Fontana di Trevi*. I must throw in a coin before I leave. Oh, the Pantheon. What about the Pantheon? Is it still open?"

"We will go see it all, yes."

"Then back to your place where we will do it all night, no sleep." I rub my hand across his body, grabbing at him, and he plunges his tongue back into my mouth. We kiss as if forbidden.

****

Jennifer

My daughter jumps out of the kid mobile without a word and doesn't look back. "Well then. Don't mind me. Guess you want me to follow." She gives no response to my snarky comment. I hate attending school functions on Saturdays.

A Jeep pulls in right next to my family truckster and parks. My heart stops. "Holy shit taco." Dean jumps out and runs to catch up with me. I thought his ex-wife had the kids this weekend. "Ugh," I whisper to the pavement and fiddle with my pink scarf. I don't want to deal with my lusty Dean yearnings at a school play. I blocked his number after I told him it was over, but I keep thinking about him and his rock-hard body.

His kids run into the school with my daughter. "Hey, Jennifer, wait up. Why didn't you text me back? Did I do something to upset you?"

"I can't deal with you right now, Dean. Listen to me. No more fucking."

"Oh, okay. I get it, though I thought we were friends first. We always make each other laugh." He combs his longish hair out of his eyes with his hand, and my fingers itch to touch his soft locks again.

"Well, shit, Dean." Close to the front door now, I whisper, "Why do I feel like I broke up with you?"

"Sorry. I don't mean to make you uncomfortable. Can we get together and talk? Later today? Come on, Jennifer. I don't want to lose our friendship. Meet me at Filtered for coffee."

"Filtered? Are you insane? Half the school moms pop in there. No way."

"My house then. No one else is around later. The kids go to their mom's after the show. I'll make coffee. We can talk. Then, you can move on. I only want to talk."

I hesitate, and my stomach grips in knots.

"At least give me ten minutes of your time."

"Yeah, okay." I scan through my planner, knowing I will regret this decision. "I'll come by late this afternoon around four."

****

At three forty-five p.m., he opens his front door barefoot, in worn jeans, no shirt, and carrying a glass of wine. He doesn't play fair.

"Dean, you changed the plan? Remember it's just a cup of coffee. You cooking dinner topless is something else entirely." I take a few steps back gesturing to his bare chest.

"Whoa, wait. Don't freak. I cook every night and opened a bottle of wine for my soup. I spilled a little on my shirt. Plus, you can't let a nice red go to waste. Might as well drink it. Please, come in."

I walk in and stop. I will not put my purse down. I need to get out of here fast, but he looks so good. "It smells amazeballs like onions and garlic."

"Spot on. The evening calls for onion soup and fresh bread. The timer should go off any minute. Come into the kitchen while I add a pinch of thyme."

I follow like a puppy and stare at those broad shoulders. I glance down at my dress. It's casual, but come on, I put it on because I look great in it. The scoop neck dress shows a tiny bit of cleavage. He hands me a glass of red as I step into the kitchen. He poured both glasses before I arrived. I take it and lean against the kitchen counter as he adds salt, thyme, and a bit more wine to the pot. The fresh herbs meet my nose.

"Smells wonderful." I melt watching the man cook and put my scarf on the counter.

"Soup is my specialty. I can't really cook, but I love a great pot of soup and fresh bread."

"Dean…"

He interrupts by brushing my hair back behind my

shoulders. "You look beautiful. Want to sit?"

I don't take even a small sip of the wine and set the glass down. "No, I won't stay long." I stare at the tile floor not wanting to see his disappointed face. He moves in front of me. His sexy chest hits at eye level if only I looked up. "Really, we need to stop fooling around. I can't even…"

My words disappear as he trails his hand along my waist and down to my hips. I meet his eyes. He kisses me, slow and gentle. I tingle in all the right places. I want this man. He thinks I'm beautiful, and it feeds my damaged mom ego. He pushes his tongue inside my mouth tasting of wine and warm man.

"Hmmmmm," I hum, not meaning to, and forget I must end things.

"Let me touch you. I want your beautiful body in my mouth, just one more time."

"Dean." I can barely get his name out. I rasp silently for air. I attempt to stay still and not wriggle out of my dress, but I officially vibrate with the need for him. "Well, fuck, Dean. What should I do? You know I want you, but this is complicated. I don't want a mess."

"We make each other laugh. We want to fuck each other. I love being inside you. Let's keep doing whatever this is between us."

He lifts me onto the kitchen counter and drags my dress up little by little exposing my thighs. I shiver knowing what he will find underneath. My rationalization to go out without undergarments was to rid myself of panty lines. In truth though, it makes me powerful and sexy.

The dress moves to my waist, and he says, "Oh, Jennifer, imagining you walking around with nothing on under here gets me instantly hard. I love it." He gives me a soft lick, and his hands slide down my thighs.

I lean back, lapping up the attention and his warm tongue inside me. I peek and protest when he stops. He lifts me off the counter with his devilish smile and leads me by the hand.

His bedroom overflows with books. They live on every surface except the navy clad bed. I soften to this sexy, geeky guy who reads and cooks. I crawl up on his bed and sink into the mattress. He wriggles behind me. I reach for his zipper. "No. Let's take care of you first," he whispers.

My eyebrows rise to my bang line. He rolls me over and begins massaging my tight shoulders. He pushes on a knot and my sore muscles.

"Ohhhhh, shit. You feel so…ohhhhh." I fall further into his rumpled sheets. He trails his hands down my lower back and works out a painful spot I didn't know existed. The movement relaxes me.

"Don't stop your magic hands. Where did you learn to do this?"

"Shhh, let me work out your tension. Just relax." He leans in trailing kisses as his hands continue to manipulate my muscles.

My eyes droop as exhaustion takes over my body. I fight the need to sleep. He continues to rub and flames of desire flare. I follow his lead and let him take care of me. If this is the way Dean treats his woman, it will be impossible to walk away. The next thing I know, his finger moves inside my wetness, massaging in ways to create a quick release. His tongue nips me elsewhere, and I writhe in pleasure as I climax.

"Ohhhhh." My face smashes on the pillow and muffles my voice. "Dean, those fingers work magic. You possess a magic finger wand." I giggle and let go of my body.

I tingle all over and beg him to stop and keep going faster in the same sentence. I orgasm again, and my skin becomes too sensitive to be touched for a few minutes. Multiple orgasms without doing much work are new to me.

Dean leaves the room. I lift myself up to get dressed but fail. The soft sheets and gentle fan lulls me a few minutes more. With two wine glasses in hand, Dean enters still clad in jeans, no shirt, and a smile.

"Feeling better?"

"Ha, never better. Thank you. I guess I'm an uptight mess. I didn't realize the situation was extreme, though."

He crawls into bed handing me a glass. "Here, this will help, too. Tell me what's going on. I know Jake's an asshole making you suffer. Something more in the works?"

Everything pours out of my relaxed body. "Yes, my marriage sucks, a total fucking mess, obviously. I keep wondering if I can leave Jake to start a new life or run away from the one I created. I want my kids, I do. I adore them, but I'm trapped. You understand?"

Dean kisses the top of my head. "Yes, I know you love them."

"I'm stuck with Jake and no job. On top of this sexless, boring housewife life filled with parenting, I quit the work I loved a hundred years ago. No recent job equals unmarketable skills to any decent PR firm. I'll need money, and it's impossible to find work with no new experience or nothing recruiters consider valuable. I doubt my resume looks decent with PTA stats and volunteer service. Employers laugh at people like me much less give me an interview. I don't know what to do."

Dean plays with my hair and listens without revealing a hint of his emotions. He doesn't offer advice either, only nods his head. We drink in silence, each of us in our own headspace but close together.

Chapter Thirteen

Jennifer

I throw on a low-cut dress, lift my boobs in place, and stare at myself in the mirror. I pucker my lips and apply a vibrant red. After I check the AT&T guy off my to-do list, I'm immobilized over my next move, but know I need to keep going. The adventure bug calls.

I rub my lips together as I walk into our living room. Jake, once again, lies on the sofa in front of the TV with a beer in one hand and the remote in the other. I watch him in silence waiting for him to acknowledge me. Instead, he nods off then burps himself awake. Super sexy. Only nine p.m. and the kids sleep soundly upstairs. Time for me to go out instead of crawling into bed with a book, like I usually do.

"Extra book club tonight. I lost track of time. Home in a few hours."

Jake jerks awake. "Okay." He rubs his crusty eyes. I grab my car keys and notice him stare at me cross-eyed. "Hey, you're really dressed up for book club."

"Yup. The meeting is at some new place downtown, so I want to look nice. You know how everyone dresses up at these wine bars. Women dress up for other women," I lie to his face. I spout off bullshit without thinking.

"Oh." He burps again and focuses back on the

ballgame.

****

I head down the almost empty interstate and realize I don't want to sit in a local brewery or wine bar. I want something outside of my comfort mom zone. In college, I went dancing, attended parties, poetry slams, plays, concerts, or hung out with friends.

Back then, I filled my planner with social engagements. Now, I schedule time to do laundry. Even in my first years at the company, I took clients out all the time. Not anymore. That cultured life doesn't even seem like mine anymore.

For years, I begged Jake to take dance lessons with me. My darling husband scoffed at me. The discussions ended before I began my pleas.

I attended a friend's fancy wedding with him a few years into our marriage, and he refused to step onto the dance floor. He sat at the assigned table by himself guarding a table of purses, and I spent the entire night dancing with a dateless groomsman. I felt lucky to dance with a partner instead of bopping to the beat alone.

The advertisements for ballroom dancing say you don't need a partner and feel free to come alone, but I can't imagine the humiliation of showing up solo. Even in my college days, I didn't do anything by myself. I'd drag Anna along or organize a group of friends. Not tonight though. Tonight, I shed my fear of embarrassment and go for it. Tonight, I will dance alone with everyone watching.

The dance studio on Broadway and Fifth Street resides in a hipster part of the city, full of young people in their early twenties. I luck out and park a few blocks away from the studio on the street front. Bright lights spill out from the wide windows in front of the building, and a white awning welcomes dancers as you step inside.

The room opens into a large space with scratched and dented hardwood floors. Cold air hits me as I step further into the room and search for someone in charge. I stop in the middle of the room, not sure where to go. Everyone gathers in big clumps chatting away and laughing like old friends.

A tall man in tight black pants stands at an old school stereo with huge speakers and stacks of CDs. I smile, glad for a fellow old school CD user. Maybe the hipsters swung back to them already?

Tall man turns abruptly as a fast tune starts. "Okay, beautiful dancers. Let's start tonight with a simple tango. Anyone needing beginner dance help, please step to the left. The rest of you, grab your favorite partner."

I step to the left and silently pray I won't be alone. Luckily, ten young people gather around me. They catch the beat and begin moving their hips to the music.

"All right," the tall man says, clapping his hands as he walks toward us. "This thrills me. I'm Mark, and I love seeing new faces. Welcome." I blush as Mark scans the crowd. His eyes stop on me, perusing my body. I can't help it. I glance down to make sure I didn't forget something big like clothes.

Mark's beautiful body sends a thrill down my spine. His pale skin and bright green eyes accent his black hair flopping over in large, soft curls. My body reddens as he focuses on my hazel eyes.

"Grab a partner," he announces to the group while heading straight toward me. Seizing my hips firmly in his hands, he says, "Everyone, watch my feet for a minute." He pulls me closer to him. I almost pant. His hard body presses tight into mine. "Just follow my lead. It's not hard," Mark whispers.

"Might be for me," I mumble, realize what I said, and flush red again. I die inside as he sweeps across the floor, practically dragging me with him. This is way out of my comfort zone.

Mark departs to help two laughing women paired together and missing every dance step. Before he leaves, he whispers in my ear, "I hope you come to class again. You aren't just a pretty thing, you have great moves, too. Keep shaking those mighty hips."

The hour flies by in an instant. I meet a lot of new and experienced dancers who smile and accept my ignorance when I don't know the steps. At the end of the last song, everyone gathers in clumps leaving me standing alone. Unsure of what to do, I meander outside to my parking spot in a dance-filled daze.

Sitting in the van, I check my text messages.

One waits from the PTA president.

—School picture forms due tomorrow.—

Delete. I already took care of it. Two more texts from the kids.

—Mom, can I take a cupcake in my lunch tomorrow?—

Fingers fly as I reply probably an hour too late.

—Please don't touch the container on the counter. They are for the bake sale. Some decorated and boxed on the top right shelf for you in the fridge. Labeled with your name.—

Next one I don't answer.

—Sarah won't get off the computer.—

I scan through my emails and officially delay the drive home. I flip through my planner and scan my to-do list. I really need to get home and finish the flyers for the bake sale. I start the car, drive out of the parking spot, and stop at the intersection.

My turn signal blinks to the right and the way home, but I can't force myself to go. Too wound up and giddy for home, I steer the opposite direction. Plus, the kids sleep safe in bed, and Jake is with them. I don't need to head home right now, restless energy pushes me further into town toward nightlife.

I should explore a club for our writing adventure. Can I score a guy in a bar? Anna's experience at C-20 amazed me, but her sex toy victim and his texts scare me senseless. Internet dating on crazy Match or Tinder make the hookup list, but the swipe this, reject that, worries me. Would my non-tech-savvy self get busted dating online? Certain to get caught on apps, this sexual, I mean writing, exercise for me won't include the internet.

A loud honk shakes me from my thoughts. I wave and drive faster to the pub district. I flip the signal to the left and whip the family truckster onto the interstate. The hipster bars around the dance studio are too cool and young for my liking. I need something with a larger, diverse crowd. I head straight to Zenos, my mid-twenties go-to spot before kids. Not too club-like but still built with a large space for bands to perform and dancing. It fits the bill.

In the dark parking lot, I adjust my scarf in the mirror and add more red lipstick. A loud thumping beat greets me. Outside, the disgruntled bouncer takes my five-dollar cover charge and doesn't act like I'm out of place. Maybe I'll fit in with this crowd. The dark room and thick air suffocate me.

I loosen my scarf. I expected drunks at this hour, but a quick scan shows a mix of people, not just overindulged college kids. The band finishes a set as I hop onto a wooden bar stool. It swivels so I rock my hips back and forth like a kid on a Sit n' Spin until I almost fall off.

An older man next to me smiles and leans toward me invading my personal bubble. His breath reeks of beer and fried food. "Hey, the bartender ignores women. You want me to yell a drink order for you?"

"No, thanks. I'm in no hurry." What should I get if he takes my order? I don't want to drink but asking for a soda makes me look lame and uptight.

"Fred, and you are?" The stinky man leers near me again. A crest of hair circles his bald head. His nose beams red and bulbous. Drunk seems his usual state.

"Hi, Fred," I say but move my body away to dissuade him.

"No name?" He grabs my hand in his sweaty palm and holds it a beat too long. I pull away and wipe it on my dress.

Fred angles closer, and spit hits my face as he talks. I pull back. He misses my uninterested hints. His squinty eyes narrow, and his half-untucked shirt hangs over his large belly as he rubs it like a pregnant woman. "Geez." I mutter out loud then say, "Ugh, no name for you tonight. I'm meeting someone. I don't think he's arrived yet." I swivel around like I expect a friend to show up at any moment.

"Hey, babe." I spin left and a good-looking man stands beside me. He appears to be my age and wears a three-piece suit. “Sorry, it took me so long to get here. I couldn’t cut out earlier from the office dinner.” He turns to the still leering Fred, then bends down to kiss my cheek. His eyes narrow toward Fred. “Excuse me, do I know you?”

“No.” Fred swings around and slides off his stool.

“Thank you so much,” I silently mouth and smile at my savior.

“No problem. I saw him do the same thing to three other women. He’s on the prowl tonight. Consider saving you my community service for the day.”

I laugh. “Well, thanks again.”

My savior turns back to his group and chats with them. I fiddle with my shirt sleeve and then my scarf. I’m not sure what to do here alone. Friends gather in close groups. The young bartender saddles up to me. “Need a drink? What can I get you?”

Savior leans into the bar beside me making eye contact with the bartender. Fred was right. The bartender had no intention of serving me. “Yeah, another beer for me, and she wants a Tom Collins tonight.”

I nod my head as the bartender mixes my drink. Savior disappears again to his friends. I don’t know where to focus. I catch a woman’s eye two bar stools down from me, and she looks away with a frown.

Think, think, think…shit. What should I do? I want to pull a book from my purse. Can I sit at the bar with a drink and read or is that socially unacceptable? Shit, in my youth I’d already be on the dance floor. I can’t believe I considered reading. Instead, I search the other direction for someone approachable. No luck. I dig in my purse but stop myself. A book in a bar screams librarian, not sexy. I want to draw men in not repel them. I text Anna.

—Hey. I'm at a bar and feel stupid. How the hell did you do this? Tips? Help? Shit. SOS.—

Anna gets back to me on WhatsApp.

—Ciao, you are too funny. Relax. Order a drink. No SOS. Sit there and chill. Give yourself one drink and if nothing happens, leave. Don't pull out a book. I know you hid one in your purse. Right?—

—Shit, yes. Of course, I have a book with me.—

Two books, I want to tell her but refrain. I never leave the house without a book. At the age of ten, a massive car accident delayed a family vacation to Florida. We were stuck on the freeway for five hours in the sweltering heat on the way to the ocean. My parents argued the whole time. The miserable day was saved by the new novel I brought.

—Put your phone down and sit there. Drink the girly drink you ordered like you mean it. Texting on your phone says, stay away.—

—Okay. Thanks.—

I put my phone down for two seconds before typing back.

—Wait. Why do you think I ordered a girly drink?—

—Whatever. Just a guess. You can do this, Jennifer. You're brilliant.—

—So glad I can still reach you.—

—Ciao.—

I repeat my mantra in my head throughout each sip of my girly Tom Collins. I can do this. Anna did this. I can do this. Anna did this.

Savior glances my way again and smiles with a

wink. I hate getting pity attention. The confident voice in my head waivers and goes crazy. He thinks you're an old lady. Your spots of gray hair make you ugly. Fuck, I shouldn't have eaten those chips at lunch.

"Hey, can I sit with you?" my savior whispers over my shoulder.

I turn toward him and smile.

"You seem a little out of your element. Is your date on the way? Or was it a story to keep the Spitter away from you?"

I nod my head yes and rack my brain for something clever to say. He looms above me, so tall, like a modern Mr. Darcy staring down at me. Not brooding but he's rugged and strong in his rumpled work suit and tie.

"Bars aren't my usual scene either. I came after work with some of my office mates. They call it bonding time. It's rude to say no to their invitations every time."

I smile and mess with my scarf. He seems nice but probably not sex project material. Then he surprises me.

"You keep drawing me in. Since you aren't expecting anyone, is there any chance you want to go somewhere else?"

"Somewhere else with me?" I ask.

"Clearly, I'm not good at this. I just got a divorce and started dating. I meant somewhere quieter where we don't need to scream to talk. Maybe grab some food at the diner on the corner?"

"Hungry but not for food." I bounce back. "But if you live nearby?" Holy fuck, did I say that out loud? This guy could be Ted Bundy. I've lost my marbles. Just because he looks nice, I'll let him take me home? But taking chances is my modus operandi tonight.

I jump off the stool, grab my Savior's hand, and drag him behind me. He yells and waves to his group of office buddies. One of them makes a joke and everyone laughs. I don't hear it but think it's best. I'm sure the punchline includes me, and it might make me change my mind.

Out on the quiet sidewalk, my Savior says, "I'm Sam, and I'll be your tour guide this evening."

"Didn't know I needed a guide." I laugh. "But please, lead the way."

Sam takes his job seriously and mutters facts about the neighborhood. The tour continues up to his apartment which he describes as a war zone inside but a fine specimen of the city. His genuine effort to connect is sweet in a first date kind of way. We walk together through his mostly empty loft to the living room space. There I drop my purse on a chair and sink into the sofa.

After he pours me a glass of red wine, I take hold of the stem without taking a sip. I need to keep my wits about me and not drink any more alcohol tonight.

"Thank you. I love your place. It's so quiet here."

"I noticed the ring on your finger. Are you married?" he asks.

"Well, it's a long story and not worth spending our time on right now." I lean in hoping he will make a move. He smells like musk and citrus, and I want more of it. I inch toward him. He might be in the throes of divorce, but he seems confident and sure of himself.

Instead of kissing me, he gently picks up the end of my hair and twirls it in his fingers. He leans closer and strokes my cheek. Soft and intimate, my body heats and yearns for more. Signaling such, I tilt forward and almost collapse into him.

His lips fall on mine, warm and tender as his hand plays in my hair. “Mmm.” I hum without even meaning to make a sound. His kiss turns deeper, opening his mouth and running his tongue along my bottom lip.

My breasts begin to throb and push against him tighter encouraging him to move his hands down to my first button. He takes his time unbuttoning as his tongue continues to play on my lips. Cool air hits my chest as he slips off my shirt. It brings bliss. His tongue follows ramping it up to the next level in an instant.

“I must take off this beautiful bra. Okay? Your moans sound magnificent. I must hear more of them right now. I want to kiss you here.” He runs his finger over my breast and patiently waits, searching my eyes for confirmation before he dives in. Taking his time, his tongue licks around my nipple inch by inch.

I figure out where on my sexy time victim checklist this man will fit. A stranger? Check. As he runs his hands down my waist, all thoughts of the list or the book fly out of my mind. He says something, but I miss it.

“Yes?” he says again a little louder. “I want you to say yes.”

“Um.” I can’t possibly come up with an answer to his question.

“If you don’t want to, we won’t, but I need to know now. You feel so soft, and I have protection so don’t worry. I bought a brand new box of condoms. They’re in my bedroom.”

I lift a brow. “You think we will need a whole box?”

“I hope so,” he whispers, kissing my earlobe.

“Yes, then.” I stand, and he leads me to his mostly

empty bedroom. Gray sheets and a navy comforter tumble off the unmade bed. I step over unpacked moving boxes scattered across the concrete floor. Obviously, he is newly divorced.

He sheds his clothes, throwing his beautiful suit on a box. I smile and follow his lead. He smirks at us both in our underwear. “I must be honest. I haven’t done this with a new person in a really long time. I was married and faithful for twelve years. I’m unsure for some reason.”

“Oh,” I chirp so loud it bounces off the empty walls. Holy taco. “We don’t have to do this if you don’t want to.” My face turns pink. Now, that I’m almost naked, he isn’t interested. Fuck, those damn potato chips again.

“Oh, no, no. I want to be with you. I just want you to understand in case…Oh God, I messed this up completely, didn’t I?” He buries his face in his hands.

“I didn’t think it was wrong before. It seemed more than right to me. How about we start where we left off?” I step toward him.

His shoulders relax, and he drags me by the hand to his bed. “I want to touch you everywhere.”

“Mmm…” I remain speechless as he peels off my panties and runs his nose and lips up my thighs. His tight muscles flex as he moves up and down my body sending shivers through my spine. My body vibrates from his attention, and it won’t take long for me to climax. His tongue dips, licking my breasts, and I find myself lifting off the bed a little.

He leaves for a moment. I open my eyes to him rolling a condom on and sliding into my wet center. He isn’t big, but he knows what to do with it. We create a rhythm between us. He moans loud ready to release. My pleasure builds as he rubs in gentle circles. I buzz, and my body explodes. We orgasm together.

Why don't all men know this trick? It should be taught in health class. As he collapses onto me, I realize he doesn't know my name.

Chapter Fourteen

Anna

My bag sits next to the door. I can't believe how quickly the days with Allessandro melted away. It seems like yesterday when we first met at his shop. Yet it was days ago. Days filled with him and me in bed together, long baths, massages, *vino*, delicious food, and walks through Rome.

Allessandro works in the kitchen, packing away dinner for me. He wants me to eat well and avoid airplane food. I twirl my hair as he places the pasta in a to-go container. He grinds some *Parmigiano* over the dish and sprinkles fresh basil. He wraps *prosciutto*, fresh mozzarella, and crusty bread in separate pieces of tin foil before layering it into a grocery bag. A decadent chocolate éclair, purchased for this occasion, tops the parcel.

The care reminds me of Luke's special preparation for our dinner dates. He used to cook pepper-crusted filet mignon with grilled asparagus for us after putting the kids to bed, but not anymore.

Allessandro brings me the bag and says, "Get your *vino* on the plane as they won't let you take your own, the heathens."

I burst into tears.

"Oh, what is it, my darling?" He takes my hands

away from my face and guides me to sit on the sofa. He looks into my eyes.

"I don't want to go."

"I don't want you to either, such a beautiful woman." He kisses me lightly on the lips.

"Then I can stay?"

His expression changes, but his voice stays soft and steady. "Oh, darling, you'd tire of an old man soon."

"No, never. I could stay here and work in your store to keep things organized."

"Yes, it sounds lovely, but in the end, one of us will tire of the other and fight. It will turn nasty. I married my wife for that mess, and besides, you have a husband. This experience belongs to lovers. You can come back and *fare l'amore* again. I savor the idea."

"Oh." A pain grabs my heart, shattering the fantasy of escaping to this life of sex, food, and painting."

"And your children. You could never leave them, no?"

"Yes, of course." My children, my husband, and my work need me. Facing reality proves harder after this complete escape. "But I need you."

He closes his eyes and meets my lips with his tongue pushed against mine. He presses his body on me and rubs my breasts. "Stay sexy. Don't forget." He doesn't love me. I take a deep breath. Whatever.

I push him away and examine his eyes. I do not matter to him. I'm just another lover, someone to play with for a week.

Hands run up my thighs, under my skirt, and tear at my panties. I don't stop him but submit. He rubs my core with his hand. I moan. He stops and returns with a condom. His pants drop, but he doesn't remove them or his crisp white shirt. I stay dressed, too. Kneeling, his tongue licks up and down and around in some pattern he perfected from years of seduction.

The tension builds, and my body tingles for more. No fancy moves this time, we just straight-up do *it.* He orgasms and swears in Italian.

He puts his pants on and tosses the condom out in the bathroom trash. I pull up my panties. He sits next to me and stares into my eyes. Soft kisses come first and then linger with his tongue. "I enjoyed these days with you. I will never forget them, my darling."

"Yes, me, too." The pain in my heart returns. I care more for him than he does for me.

"The taxi will arrive at any moment." He stands up and holds out his hand. I take it, and he grabs my bag. I carry his thoughtfully prepared dinner. "You packed everything? Purse, passport, wallet, money?"

"Yes, all here." I tap my fake Louis Vuitton bag and my passport falls out of the top. I shove it back in among the other junk.

"Then we shall go." We descend the narrow staircase and go outside. The taxi waits. Allessandro opens the door and places my suitcase in the trunk. He leans into the cab and kisses me for the last time. "Remember. Screw, food, paint, and write every single day."

"Every single day."

He shuts the door and the taxi drives off. Tears stream down my cheeks as the driver battles through rush hour to arrive at the airport. I can't leave my children, but I want Allessandro to desire me as much as I long for him.

****

Jennifer

"Just get in the van, now please, or we will be late," I beg up the stairs.

"Coming. Coming," their two voices chorus back.

"No phones. Leave those evil things at home." My son descends the stairs with his phone in hand and his face glued to it.

"Holy Taco, Kevin, did you hear me? Sweet child of mine, I will ground you."

"Oh, Mom, you need to calm down. No need to hurry." My son pats me on the shoulder while he tosses his phone onto the couch.

"Let's go," I repeat heading outside.

Coffee and thinking about dance class tonight is the only thing getting me through the morning. This feistiness makes me hopeful, so I text Jake.

—Hey, wanna come to dance class with me tonight and shake your booty?—

No response from him all afternoon. I take the kids to their soccer practice and dance class before heading back home to make dinner. Jake walks in as I set eggplant parmesan on the table.

"Hey, you didn't text me back today. I would love for you to come to dance class with me. Will you?" His face pinches, and I hold my breath.

He glances around the kitchen and at the kids helping me place napkins on the table. "Uh. No. Too tired and the game's on," Jake says and keeps his eyes on the kids.

I stare at him, to communicate something other than the words I want to say. "I'd really like for you to join me tonight. It's fun, and I promise they don't make you feel silly or foolish for not knowing the moves. Everyone welcomes newcomers."

After a moment, his gaze meets mine. "I said no, Jennifer. I worked hard all day long for this life you want. Why do ya gotta push me all the damn time, woman? You never stop."

"I thought you might want to go with me and do something fun for a change," I bark back at him.

"Shit, Jennifer. Why do ya control everything? Why can't ya leave it alone?"

"Leave what alone exactly, Jake? You? Our marriage? Your attitude?" The kids leave the room sensing a fight.

"Yes. Me. Leave me alone. We can't afford fun time anymore. You created this life instead." His hands splay around the kitchen.

"What do you mean this life? I created this life? We had children and bought this house together."

He shakes his head and backs out of the room without another word.

I breathe for five minutes to calm down. "Everybody, dinner," I call out. Jake doesn't come. Instead, the front door slams. Shit, I can't help it, my first thought turns to dance class. I don't want to miss it.

After I clean the dinner dishes and update the calendar for tomorrow, I walk into the living room to find Jake on the sofa with the TV remote in hand.

"I'm not gonna fight and waste my time with ya, Jennifer." He keeps his eyes on the stupid baseball game.

"Okay," I say. "Time for dance class. See you later."

I turn off the mom-mobile radio and barrel down the highway toward the dance studio. "I guess this is how divorce happens. It slides up on you without a warning," I say out loud. I need to rid myself of this stomach pain. Fighting with Jake causes severe distress. Saying the word divorce out loud clenches at my stomach even more. It may happen this time.

My parking spot from the class before stands empty, waiting for me. I jump out of the mommy jalopy in my high heels. "Alone and divorced," I say. The knot in my stomach shrinks a little. I spin the words in my mouth as I saunter into the bright studio.

Once there, I shake myself out of the divorce thought cycle and glance down at my new white dress. I mirror sexy Marilyn Monroe tonight. I sport the curves, so I assumed I could rock them, but now the other dancers stare at me with tight smiles. Standing alone, it seems like a spotlight focuses on me. I look around.

The people in attendance and the dance moves are different. They act like old friends and jump into the complicated dances without instruction. I watch them samba a minute before I bolt toward the safety of my mom van. Mark, the instructor from the week before, slides between me and the front door. I stop.

"Oh yum, you came back and look superhot tonight."

"Uh, yeah. But I gotta get home now." I stumble over the words. What did he mean "oh yum"? Did he just make fun of me?

"No, wait. What? Oh, I guess you didn't see the window sign last week. The second week of every month, we practice choreography studied earlier. This gives the old-timers an opportunity to come out and get their moves on. Lots of these dancers compete. Open dance week showcases their talent. Not a class to take per se as much as a free rehearsal space."

I smile and turn to leave.

He gently grabs my arm. "Wait. Don't go. Please stay. Not everyone is a professional. All performers love someone new watching them, me included. I want you to stay. Please?"

"Ugh, I feel out of place," I mumble as he grabs my waist and pulls me close.

"You smell so good tonight too, like a field of flowers. I wanna dance. You can follow my lead."

Five minutes of him pushing and pulling me around the dance floor gives me time to sink into my new role here. I learn the footsteps as he whispers them into my ear. His earthy scent and his sexy voice send a thrill down my spine. Is he interested or gay?

"You look so tight in this dress tonight," he whispers again, then sucks on my earlobe.

Holy taco, tight? Well, then. Fuck, maybe not gay. I lean into him more. Why label him? It doesn't matter. I flush, realizing I was consoling myself with the gay excuse. If he doesn't want me, it makes the rejection easier to handle. He suckles my neck. His confidence emboldens me. He runs his arm up my waist creating tingles in my stomach. Ugh, maybe he wants to calm me with sexy dance moves, and I need to get over myself.

"Um, thanks." Fuck, what did he say?

"This dress looks amazing on you."

"Well, I wanted a certain look," I answer with a loud voice and blush, realizing the other dancers notice us.

"I see and love it. We need to find you a subway grate before the night is over."

"Yeah, should be easy in Tulsa." I laugh to hide my embarrassment.

"Can you stay after and help me clean up a bit? Interested? My boyfriend will join us too if you want," he says licking the rim of my ear. I scan the room for anything out of order and find only a pile of CD cases scattered on the dance floor.

"I'd love to?" My voice hikes up a bit too high. I must write this shit in my head, so I can get it on the computer later. Okay, you can do this, Jennifer. I'll stay and let this strange scenario play out for the book, all in the name of research, of course.

Dipping me low, I notice my dance partner stare at a man across the room with red hair and arm tattoos. Their smoldering glances at one another make me queasy. I'm a prop for their jealousy. This must be his life partner.

At the end of class, I busy myself by heading to the ladies' room. I don't want the other dancers to notice me lingering. I apply more red lipstick and check my teeth. I struggle over my decision. Do I want to stay or bail from the dance studio cleaning session?

The experience of two men sounds interesting but uncomfortable. I emerge ten minutes later to find myself overdressed. Both shirtless men stand ripped with six-packs and tight pants. I no longer question my indecision.

"Seriously, is this real?" I say out loud like an idiot. No way will I share my mom belly with these hotties. I doubt neither of them know what a real mom belly looks like. I protest with a hand wave. "I'm out of here."

"But wait, darling." Red hair reaches for my hand. I let him pull me in. His heat seeps into my skin and a mixture of nausea and curiosity arouses me. "You found an older, curvy number," he says to Mark, ignoring me standing there in his arms.

I can't go through with this. "Older?" I choke out.

Mark rubs his hand up my back. "She is beautiful and experienced."

"Good cover," I say in my strict mom voice. I can mark this trio off my list. What would a reader think about my insecurity?

Dear reader, I'm now, obviously, a total and utter mess. I not only had sex with everyone near me, but also people who didn't even notice I was in the room with them.

Yep, I've fallen off the rails. Bumpers pulled, and I barrel down unchartered territory. I shove away from their toned arms, interrupting their sensual dance.

"Dance with us," Mark yells, clapping. He spins me around, clasps his hands tight onto my hips, and tugs me into his well-endowed erection. Tight pants show the outline of it jutting toward me. No longer sexy, his large cock disgusts me. I need to leave. Before I push away again, his left hand falls from my body. He grabs behind him, thrusting into his boyfriend's ass. "Oh, baby, you're ready for me," he sings behind him.

I slide out of his remaining hand hoping he won't notice, but he says, "Oh, sexy woman, you can't go. We just started class. I thought you wanted to dance. You will be a first for us, something to check off our bucket list."

"What do you mean?" Bucket list, is this a joke?

Fuck this.

"We never screwed an older mom figure. This one smells like jasmine," the partner says, sliding his hand up the side of my body. He stares at me now. "You can teach us different old school moves. Plus, Mark's mommy fetish needs to be fed."

I flush beet red, and heat rushes to my chest. "I don't think, I mean…ugh, this is not for me. I won't play the mommy game. I gotta go." I make a crazy face and run to the door.

Both men laugh as I leave, and the door bangs closed behind me. Standing outside in the dark, I watch them "clean up" the ballroom by themselves.

****

Mint tingles my tongue as I brush my teeth, standing next to Jake in our bathroom. For a moment, I flash to our earlier married years when the two of us did everything together. I place my hand on top of Jake's. Tomorrow, he leaves for a week-long business trip to California.

"Hey, wanna play with some sexy-time toys tonight?" I ask with my mouth full of foamy toothpaste.

"What did you say?" He turns and blinks at me.

I spit in the sink. "Sex toys? Tonight? I bought some. We can play with them together." I spin like a princess, trying for cute and flirty.

"Gross, no. Seriously, Jennifer? Ya bought stuff from one of those creepy stores off the highway? What ya thinking? How much money did ya spend on the sex crap?"

"Yes, it will be fun. We can shake things up a bit."

"No. Ya know I hate dirty crap. It's not right." He throws his hands up in the air. "Plus, it's an expense we don't need. I bet ya can't even return it." He leaves the bathroom, and I watch him go.

In bed, he turns his back to me and says, "I need a good night's sleep for tomorrow's meetings. I'll sleep in here tonight. Do not mess with me, Jennifer."

I hesitate before getting into bed. Should I even sleep in here? I remember the toys I hid right below us. I creep under the blanket on my side of the bed. I could really piss him off and pull them out. No. I close my eyes for what seems like forever and don't fall asleep. I lay in bed next to a snoring Jake. This restlessness won't work, so I get up and go into the living room. Tonight, I'm the one who sleeps on the couch.

Chapter Fifteen

Anna

My stomach aches. The last time I felt this way, I left home for college and missed my mom and dad. I want Allessandro. Nothing will fix this longing to touch him. The fact he doesn't want me makes the hurt throb more. I keep my emotions under the surface with thoughts of my beautiful children. I miss them.

The airplane food cart weaves down the narrow aisle. I eye the dinner Allessandro made for me. It sits tucked in its tidy little bag under the seat in front of me. I twirl my hair. My stomach growls, and I relent putting down the tray table to arrange my meal.

The man next to me, absorbed in his iPhone says, "Your lunch looks good. Better than the rubber garbage they will serve us."

"Yes, it does." I open the parcel to find a little heart-shaped note tucked inside.

Enjoy life, beautiful. Allessandro.

I bite my lip and examine the food. I don't want to break down in front of some guy I'll sit next to for seventeen hours. I stuff everything, including the note, back into the bag and clip up the tray table. I bolt to the lavatory.

Both bathrooms occupied, I wait in the aisle behind a chatty American woman. She asks me questions and tells me about her recent tour, Europe in ten days, hitting all the major sites. They just adored it. She still wears the matching fluorescent yellow T-shirt their tour guide gave them. I want to get away and be alone for a moment. I smile and nod politely but tell her off in my head.

An older gentleman exits the bathroom on the left. He creeps out of the stall, and his cane sticks to the folding door, which results in a nail-biting contest between the American tourist and the grandpa to negotiate the use of the restroom.

I let out a deep breath when the two leave and take a moment of peace. The bathroom on the right opens. Moving away from the aisle to let the occupant out, I glance up at him. The thirty-year-old man with blondish hair and a nice tan smiles at me. I swoon at his true-blue eyes.

He notices me stare at him. "You want company?" he says in a French accent. He pauses in the doorway and tilts his head back beckoning me toward him, only a second to choose. The thought of him touching me makes my head swim. I glance left and right and find no one paying attention. I step into the bathroom. He leans forward and slides the door lock to occupied. It turns on the little bathroom light.

"*Bonjour,* lovely lady. American?"

"No." I lie.

"Where are you from?"

"*Roma.*"

"*Italiano.*"

"*Sì.*"

He caresses my face with his hands and brings his mouth toward mine. He tastes of cigarettes and chocolate. At his touch, my mind melts away and all thoughts of Allessandro disappear. I need more contact. I greedily put my hands on his waist and squish into him. I bury my head into his chest and inhale his earthy musk.

With little space to move, we stand close. He nibbles at my bottom lip which sends a thrill down my body. It is not enough. Running his hands down my sides, they find my bottom. He squeezes and presses his pelvis against mine.

The plane hits turbulence, and the fasten seatbelt sign pops on with a ting. The captain's voice comes over the intercom. "It will get a little bumpy. Please return to your seats," she says.

"We go?" I ask in a fake Italian accent.

"No." He kisses my neck and unbuttons my blouse. His mouth tastes my cleavage, and his teeth pull down my corset exposing my breasts. I run my hands under his T-shirt around his strong pecs with little hair.

The plane bumps and knocks him on top of me as I stumble back over the toilet. He laughs and so do I. It's really cramped in here. How does anyone ever do *it* on a plane? We readjust, and he slides down to the floor. He grabs my legs and runs his hands up my thighs. He lifts my skirt and dives under.

A knock on the door makes us freeze. "Excuse me," a voice from the door says, "You really need to head back to your seat now."

"*Mademoiselle*, I feeling not so well. How do you say…I feel like vomit? The bumps make me ill." He fakes a gag. I cover my mouth to suppress a giggle.

"Oh, okay, sir. Get back to your seat as soon as you can."

He fakes vomits again. “I will.”

We wait a moment like giddy teenagers almost caught by our parents. He drags down my panties. I think about how Allessandro was there a few hours earlier. The moment my French stranger’s tongue finds me, I forget the heart pain. My body smolders until I climax.

“My turn,” he says and stands. I kneel and undo the zipper of his tight jeans. His tool falls out. I touch him with my mouth, and he moans an approval. He makes demands of me in French. I don’t know what he says, but he kisses my neck, and I play with him.

Yanking me closer to him, he takes out a condom from his wallet. He slides the rubber on and flips me over. I lean on the sink with my backside out. My legs spread as far as they will go in this tiny space. He shoves inside me, and we moan.

His fingers grab at my breasts, and he watches us in the small, smudged mirror. I stare too as he pushes into me and groans. His body exits mine, and he tosses the condom into the mini trash can trap door. I return my panties to their rightful place and straighten my tousled hair. Pants zip up, and he tucks in his black T-shirt.

His body presses against mine. Our warm lips meet. “What’s your name?”

“Anna. You?”

“Julien. We wait until the fasten seatbelt sign turns off or everyone will stare.”

“Okay. You’ve done this before?”

“Once or twice.” His eyebrows rise up and down. “Your accent sounds American now.”

“Whatever. I tried to be exotic.” I bite my bottom

lip.

"Exotic?" He shrugs, contemplating. "Not bad for someone older."

"For an old lady?"

"Yes, no, don't twist words. You're getting me in trouble." He presses his lips on mine and kisses me until the turbulence passes.

****

After going through customs, I wait at the international baggage claim. The luggage dumps out onto the conveyor belt. Julien smiles from across the way. I smile back but cringe when he holds the hand of the woman beside him. "Idiot," I mumble. What am I thinking? I did the same thing, didn't I?

I take my black bag when it drops. It feels as heavy as my stomach. Leaving Allessandro hurts more than I imagined possible. Even after the escapade with the Frenchman in the bathroom, I long for Allessandro. An uncontrollable urgency to be touched envelopes my body.

Back in Tulsa, I need to cover my tracks. I find the baggage claim from Atlanta and my writing conference. After a search on my phone, I remove flight stickers from my bags and head over to the United domestic area for my pretend arrival. I chose a flight arriving later than my actual flight from Rome to beat the family there without question. Now, though, I wait alone stuck in my own thoughts for at least an hour.

I sit with my bags and watch passengers collect their luggage and meet up with their loved ones. My gaze follows a handsome, tall guy with curly hair. He looks Italian. I examine every inch of him wondering about his naked body. I want to follow him back to his rental car and *do* him in the back seat. Brilliant.

Damn, what is wrong with me? The only moment in the last ten hours I didn't suffer was when Julien touched me, kissed me, *did* me. I want the same attention again now. I need it to free my mind of Allessandro, his lips, and his voice.

I pick up the phone, dial his number, and twirl my hair. I stare at the large red send button and do nothing. He doesn't want to talk to me. Oh, to be in the 1980s again just for a moment so I could call and only listen to his voice without stalking him. Damn caller ID. Whatever. The seconds tick by as I picture him cooking, massaging me in the shower, buying flowers, and kissing my neck.

I text Jennifer.

—Ciao. I landed a few minutes ago. Waiting for Luke to pick me up.—

She replies immediately.

—Thank all gods you came home. I feared you might stay forever.—

—I thought about it, but the kids…—

—Yeah. I get it. Hope you had a great time. Can't wait to hear everything.—

—Coffee soon?—

—Fuck yeah.—

After about an hour, I locate my family across the airport. Brooklyn sports different shades of pink, and Ben wears pants mysteriously too short for him, again. They spot me through the crowds and run into my arms, yelling, "Mommy."

My arms stretch as big as my smile. I hold them tight and savor the smell of sunshine on their necks. I want to weep for my betrayal. Of course, I could never leave but thinking about staying hurts, too. They bounce around the airport.

Luke stands back until the kids finish, takes my bags, and pecks me on the cheek. “Hello. Did you have a good trip?”

“Yep.” How did he become a stranger? Unshaven and disheveled, he looks like he slept in his clothing. His eyes flutter with the same long, caring lashes I love.

“Did the kids beat you up?”

“Yeah.” He smiles. Damn, I forgot his smile. What happened to us?

Chapter Sixteen

Jennifer

The next morning, Jake doesn't speak to me. He kisses each kid goodbye and says he loves them. "Love you too, Daddy," they respond robotically back at him as he walks out the door.

I bend over and pick up a kid's dirty sock on the kitchen floor. "Can you guys please not leave socks everywhere?" I yell at seven in the morning taking my anger out on them. Fuck. "Dirty socks in my kitchen makes me crazy." Or crazier.

"Okay, Mom," Kevin says and flashes his dimple at me. "Do we have any Kashi cereal?"

In the pantry, I take their favorite breakfast food from the top shelf and lean against the door jam. Opening the Tupperware container, I replenish the cereal. Thinking of Jake not saying goodbye to me makes my eyes water. I pull the cardboard box apart so it will lay flat and add it to the recycling bin. Fighting is better than ignoring one another. Not speaking to me means he has no feelings left for us.

The school bus picks the kids up, and I go to my computer to pay a few bills. I get a pop-up advertisement of a blue, talking bunny, "Everyone's Favorite Toy," and remember my own sex toys wrapped in a towel, untouched, and hidden under my bed. I can't seem to find the time to play with them, much less read the directions on how to use them.

My planner lays before me taunting. The chores can wait. Luckily, I bought batteries in all sizes at the store earlier this week because I wasn't sure which size I needed. I looked like a weirdo woman throwing six of every battery in the cart.

I pull out the toys, rip the packages open, and throw the trash at my feet cluttering the room like a child at Christmas. Staring at the mess on the floor stops me. Fuck it. Everything doesn't need to look perfect all the time. Sexy items line my bed in a careful row: a vibrator, nipple clamps, three different creams, and rainbow condoms.

I glance at the sheets of directions scattered and wing it. I touch the clamps and smell one of the creams. I place double-A batteries into the green vibrator and ignore the rest of the sexy time objects. Ugh, it's too much work to figure out how to use them by myself. I turn on the new Rabbit, and it buzzes in my quiet house.

The loud humming makes me peek at the open bedroom door. I change locations and streak into the bathroom. I change my mind, run back to the bed, and grab the hot pink, vibrating nipple clamps, and the Lelo Sona Cruise that advertises cruise control. It comes with a USB charging cord. Might as well try it, too.

Back in the bathroom, I lock the door, lie on the bathmat, and put the clamp on my breast. "Shit. Shit. Shit." I rip it off and throw it across the room. "Holy shit taco." A red mark circles my sore nipple and will certainly turn blue. Wait, it might be good advice for my fictional audience.

Dear Reader, clamps for your nipples hurt like hell if you don't know how to use them properly. Beware, you might bruise your boobies.

I focus on the vibrator hoping for some pain relief. Buzzing this entire time, the noise no longer shouts in my ear. I take a deep breath and allow the toy to work its magic. The release comes in an instant. I stumble back to bed and promptly fall asleep.

My phone alarm rings twenty minutes before the kid's school pick-up time. "Amazeballs." What a nap. I almost slept through the carpool line. Glad I thought ahead. Naps aren't a regular scheduled activity.

A little panic seeps in, and I want to grab my planner to check what I slept through. Instead, I thank my phone alarm, and I throw on a slinky, red dress. Glancing at myself in the mirror, I say, "It's a bit much for the school run." I bounce to the kid hauler with a feisty spring in my step. My chore lists can wait.

****

"How about ice cream?" I ask, surprising the kids.

"Really?" my littlest says, "But treats before dinner makes a bad choice, mommy."

"Today we shall do something a little wild baby."

Sitting in a small booth at the retro ice cream parlor, we lick our waffle cones. I think of Anna. I wonder about her Italian adventure. She just got back in town, and I haven't seen her yet. "Mommy, want some of my chocolate ice cream?"

"No, thanks. I bought it for you." I smile and pull her close for a snuggle.

"When you guys finish, we need to head home to take care of homework. We'll get take-out tonight, too."

"Yay," they sing. "Pizza."

I rush through bath time, homework, and phone out for dinner. The kids bounce around the house overjoyed to get both pizza and ice cream in one day. I deserve a night off from cooking and cleaning. No planner consulting for me tonight. "Okay, time for bed. Mom needs to work." I third person myself.

"Okay, goodnight, Mom."

"Love you, Mom."

"Read one more story, Mom?"

I nuzzle the little one again. "No more stories tonight. Time for me to write my own story." I must write the dance scene now, so I don't forget the details. They are too unbelievable to make up.

I boot up the computer and an old photo of our family pops up on my startup screen. I smile at the beautiful, happy picture taken on a hike of a sweaty, red-faced family. A pain hits the pit of my stomach. I open a new blank document and realize this isn't about the book anymore. The random sex isn't a symptom of my bad marriage but the result of a bad marriage. My phone pings with a text from Dean.

—Are you there? Do you still have my number blocked? I know you want me to leave you alone but can we talk?—

I cringe. I unblocked his number hoping to hear from him again. I never told him and don't respond. Ten minutes go by before he texts again.

—I think I'm pregnant.—

I crack up and dial his number. "Hey, give me a minute while I walk outside."

"Okay, I'm so glad you called. I was worried when I didn't hear from you," he says with a smile in his voice.

"So do you have morning sickness?"

"Kind of feels like it. I know this sounds insane, but I miss you." He sighs. "I really want to see you."

"You miss sex with me, you mean? You want to bump in the night again, you mean?" I sneer at him but laugh, too.

"Ha, no. Not really, I…well…I want to see you. Plus, we really need to deal with this pregnancy scare."

"Dean. I'm fixed, so it isn't mine."

"Oh, okay, you got me. Maybe I'm not pregnant."

"No kidding."

"Can we meet to talk? In a public place? I promise I just want to talk…to see you. It isn't only sex. I miss my friend."

"All right. Tonight works. Jake's out of town for work. The kids are already in bed so you can come here if you're quiet. I don't want to wake them. I planned to write, but I could pull out some new toys instead." I flirt forgetting he wanted to talk. "Maybe you can join me. Hell, maybe you can teach me how to use some of them."

"Screw talking. I'm one thousand percent in and on my way," he screams into the phone.

"Meet me in the backyard. Go through the side gate," I whisper before he hangs up.

Running inside, I debate what vibe I want to give Dean. Should I stay in my sweats and do the whole casual hanging out at home all night and you stopped by thing? Or do I want to be honest with myself and throw on something decent he will find sexy? My gaze catches on a new black number. I say to it, "A simple black dress without underthings, yes please."

****

It takes me ten steps in the backyard before my eyes semi-focus in the dark. The moonless, pitch-black sky creates a perfect secret meeting place.

"Great yard. I'm over here in the lounge chair," he whispers in the dark.

"Wow, you got here fast," I say walking barefoot in the grass.

"I was in the car and not far away. Come over here and sit with me." I follow his voice with my hand in front of me so I don't trip. Before I locate him, he pulls me down, and I center my body on top of his. Uncomfortable, I shift.

"Whoa, wait. Don't take it off yet."

"No, I'm not. I don't want to crush you. This can't be enjoyable."

He scoots over a bit making more room, and we sit in silence for a long while. He runs his hand through my hair. The breeze blows my neighbor's wind chimes, and I can't help being annoyed by the noise. The interruption jars me.

"Jennifer?" he begins with his serious voice.

I turn and kiss him, shutting down any future plans for talking. My aggressive kiss sends a clear message—no deep conversation tonight. He glides his hands up and down my sides. I marvel at his kissing ability with just enough tongue and no teeth. I fall into the moment sucking on his tongue and use my hands to arouse him.

He lifts his shirt, and I run my hands around his chest. He sighs and relaxes into my touch. It encourages me to unbutton his jeans.

I kiss his stomach and push the jeans down. "Commando tonight, huh? I like it. Always ready."

He laughs quietly. "I didn't expect anything. Well, I hoped maybe, but honestly, I ran out of clean clothes."

"Sexy." I smirk while helping him pull his pants down. He tugs off his shirt and lies on my patio furniture nude, hard, and tempting. I want to fuck his brains out and ride him until we both scream. Touching his hard cock makes me lose my mind. I might go off in a matter of seconds this time.

"Fuck." I pull away a bit.

"What's wrong?"

"Nothing. Well, yes, there is a lot wrong with this, but I want to fuck your brains out right now. I know it's wrong, but I want you bad tonight."

I sense his smile as he kisses me. His hands slowly pull the dress over my head as his mouth trails down my body with his lips. He nips at all the right places. "Commando, I see?" he says back at me with a gentle laugh.

I repeat his words, "I didn't expect anything. Well, I hoped maybe."

He deep laughs now, dragging me under him. He kisses my thighs and begins to work his way up my body.

"Wait, Dean. Don't." He stops. I look at him and say, "Okay, finish there first." He laughs again and trails his tongue like before. Swirling his tongue on each nipple feels like everything.

"I long to ride you," I whisper and giggle. "Holy shit, did I just say that out loud?"

"You did and please do. I love watching you move on me."

I climb aboard, and we merge together. "Ooohhh." I never moaned before, but lately, I've found my voice in sex. Dean's magic finger skills play a huge part when it comes to my body. He takes the other breast and pulls gently with his teeth. My body flushes with pleasure. He waits for me to take charge. I hesitate. I'm on the edge and don't want to come yet.

Dean grabs my ponytail and yanks it gently to get my attention. This wakes me from my mental orgasm. "Come on, Jenn. Let go." He plants a gentle kiss on my swollen lips.

I plant my feet next to his thighs and come apart. He orgasms with me. I climb off and pout.

He rolls to his side to face me, "Hey, what happened? What's wrong?"

"I just thought, well, I wanted it to last longer. I came too fast, and I really wanted you to come apart under me after working on it for a long time."

"Well then." He laughs a little too loud. "Let's do it again."

"Really? You could go again already?" Jake can last for about two minutes, then it's impossible to get him up and going again. One and he is done. I can't help myself. Dean is no Jake. I cackle out loud as I roll on top of him again.

Dean pushes the hair out of my face. "Jenn, of course. With you, I'm always ready to go. I don't want to hurt you if you're worn out."

"Oh my, get inside me right now. So fucking hot." I force him down and climb aboard trying to get a good angle.

The pace changes from fast fucking to affectionate caressing. I relax and ride him slow while his hands travel lightly over my body landing on my ass with a squeeze.

"Mmmmmm," I moan. My orgasm creeps, slow, and intentional. We curl together and listen to the crickets. I fall asleep for a few minutes and awaken at the touch of Dean's hand stroking my hair. I open my eyes and kiss him gently in the quiet of the night with only birds chirping in the background.

"How are you?" Dean asks.

I can't help but giggle. "Amazeballs."

"No, I mean with everything else."

"I know." I stretch out long on the lounger.

"So? How are you?"

"You mean about us or life in general?"

"Either?" He probes.

"Do you genuinely want to hear?" I gaze into his brown eyes.

"Yeah, you know I do. I know what it's like to live in an unhappy marriage. Talking to you during our soccer coaching days helped more than you know. It seems silly, but I looked forward to those few minutes a week with you. I get it, Jennifer. Terrible marriages can be hard."

"You don't want to hear about my problems." I stare at Dean straight in the face.

"I do, though. Meg was impossible to live with. I understand how hard something bad can be. If you want to talk, I want to listen."

Dean leans down and kisses me with soft lips enticing me to talk.

"I don't know how everything fell apart between us. Jake was my first love. We met in college, our senior year. Back then, I made every party happen by arranging get-togethers, always the social one. Though on the inside, I remained a young, insecure girl who had sex with my high school boyfriend, John, once in the cliché backseat of his mom's sedan. The experience horrified me." I giggle remembering the moment.

"He couldn't really get his cock inside of me. The boy couldn't find where to put it. I couldn't help him, because I too was clueless. I knew logistically how it should happen, but I wasn't sure how to help him put it there. Plus, those seats in the car didn't lend any support."

"Poor guy. Poor you." Dean leans into me further, stroking my hair.

"It was also the first time anyone had seen my privates, as my mom called them. I hadn't even heard the word vagina until one of the first nights in my dorm room at college when my brand-new roommate said to me, 'Take care of your pubic hair, girl. You plan to grow a bush down there or what?'

"Up until then, it was simply called my privates, and I was expected to keep my legs crossed and covered. God condemned anything different, and you weren't allowed to talk about it. Mom said, 'When it's time, your husband will take care of you.' For me to consider sex with my high school boyfriend, a boy so religious himself he felt guilty about the whole experience, was a huge rebellion."

"You rebel, you." Dean licks my ear lobe.

"At the time, I was worried about my virginity. I wanted to get it over and done with. After sex with John, I declared, 'Virgin be gone.' He didn't find me funny. Technically, it was an incorrect statement too as no penetration occurred."

"Hmm, what happened to dick-wounded John?" Dean asks.

"Of course, without a guilty heart, he dumped me after the pathetic car incident for Debra, a girl known to sleep around. He actually said, 'It's not you, it's me.' I told him, 'I hope she helps you figure out where to put it,' and never spoke to him again."

"Ha." Dean laughs.

"By then, all my friends had done it already. As the last virgin in my social group, it seemed weird for me to be upset or talk about the challenges, so I remained clueless.

"Then, in college, I felt insecure about my body. The freshman fifteen became the freshman twenty. I hung out with lots of guys in our friend group and flirted but didn't let anything go beyond a random kiss. I had a single one-night stand I didn't really enjoy and decided a committed relationship fit better for me.

"Then I met sweet, kindhearted Jake who wooed me. We were young and happy once. Naïve me thought our love was enough, but we didn't talk about what we wanted from life before we got married. We enjoyed our marriage until we had kids."

"I understand." Dean holds me tight. "I get it."

"Now, Jake either screams at me about money or he ignores me completely. He isn't the same mild-mannered man I married. The other night, he woke me up when he came to bed to tell me to clean the dishes. At first, I ignored him, but he was serious. He kicked me with his foot and said it again."

"What?"

"I got up confused. I had cleaned the kitchen after dinner, so there wasn't a mess. On the counter, I found three beers and some empty bowls. He wanted me to clean his snack dishes."

"Nice," Dean says with sarcasm dripping off this tongue. "He couldn't clean up after himself?"

"Guess not." I snuggle in closer. We lie there together in a collapsed heap of exhaustion until we accidentally doze off.

Dean mutters, "What the hell."

****

The cold spray of water hits my naked ass. "Shit. Shit. Shit." I jump up and more water sprays me. "We fell asleep. Luckily, the sprinkler turns on automatically at five a.m."

Instead of running to get out of the water, Dean leans over and kisses me. "Thank you, scheduled watering times. So much fun. I better go now. With you glistening in this water, I might ravage you again."

I push him away and get a breast lick which makes my insides squeeze in desire.

"Goodnight, sweetheart," he says and heads out of the yard.

I dash, wet and buck naked back inside, thanking the sprinklers for making an appearance and saving us from a tragic morning of embarrassment. In the kitchen, my bare foot hits the floor and I slide, falling on my ass and yelping out in pain. In my hurry to get my naked ass out of the early morning light, I forgot how slippery the kitchen tile is when wet. Karma is a bitch. Twisted on the kitchen floor, nude, and wet, a big smile spreads across my face as I think about Dean. No regrets.

Chapter Seventeen

Jennifer

A swirl of mist hugs manicured lawns as my feet pound past. My fast walk every morning helps me sleep. I find three miles a day breathes life into my body and keeps off the extra perimenopausal weight.

I walk the same measured route every single day and never veer from it. The unintended consequence of seeing the city I love, allows me to wave hello every morning to the same few loyal walkers and dog owners. It's a secret community of people who expect one another but don't know each other beyond our walking paths. I always walk alone for my free therapy.

I turn the corner on my regular loop when Sexy Stranger, my nickname for him, saunters toward me. This is the third day in a row I spot him. The last couple of days our eyes met, and we shared a smile. He must be an out of town visitor. We sometimes get those in the Brady Heights Historic District loop. Unlike the boring suburban houses, which all look alike, this interesting architecture draws a diverse crowd.

This tall, Sexy Stranger meanders toward me with methodical steps and in an English accent says, "Hiya."

I gape at him like an idiot, sidestep, and keep walking. Shit. Sexy Stranger wasn't supposed to speak. Now, what? Like my game with Anna, I created an insane backstory for him. In my delusion, his elderly mother died recently. Estranged from her son, she lived in Tulsa her whole life alone.

When he got the call about her death, he expected to find a hoarder's mess. In fact, his wealthy, organized mother left him her money, her historic home, and a thick envelope addressed to him. Reading her final words makes his stomach hurl, and he puts it off for another day. Every morning he obsesses over her letter while walking the loop.

Not part of my fictional story, his accent throws me. I pat the crazy bun on the top of my head and glance down at my body. Ugh, I'm a total disaster.

I don't shower, dress, or do makeup until after my morning exercise. My orthopedic running shoes protect my feet and help my nasty bunions. My outfit includes hot pink mismatched yoga clothes, a purple scarf, and a gray, mortifyingly ugly vest holding my keys, phone, and dirty snot rags. There is no way Sexy Stranger in khakis and shades just spoke to me with his charming accent.

"Shit, shit, shit, and shhhhhiiittt," I mumble remembering the victim checklist at home in my wallet. Exotic accent places number four. No wonder random hot men never spoke to me before the sex writing adventure began. Who would want to fuck this mess much less say hello?

****

I shower the next morning and color coordinate my outfit for my walk. I won't take the chance of walking by my handsome accent man in mismatched yoga pants and no makeup again. I don't want to look too done up as my Southern mother says, so I stick with the ponytail, tight shirt, and a dab of color on my cheeks. Shit, okay, I put makeup on, too. Who knows what could happen?

As I round an old tree-lined section of my walk, Sexy Stranger passes by me. He only smiles today, so I turn around and follow him. I don't know how to start a casual conversation. After a few minutes of pounding steps, he says, "Lass, you following me?"

"Uh…"

"Sorry. Should say I hope you are." He turns and winks.

"I am. But I promise I won't take your wallet." Ugh, I forgot how to flirt without sounding like a stalker.

"Don't have me wallet to nick." He holds up his empty hands. "But you could search me. I'm here a fortnight to visit your city on business and out for a stroll. Rented a flat around the corner." He points up the pathway.

"How do you find our fair city?" Holy taco, I copied his accent like a dork.

He smiles. "Bit lonely to be honest. Don't have me mates here. Aren't many tourists to chat up, and business doesn't take much of me time."

"Hmm…that stinks." I don't know what else to say. We walk next to one another for another block in silence.

"Join me for a cuppa?"

"A what?"

"Forgot gotta say it American now. Join me for a cup of tea? There's a little coffee shop around the corner there."

"Uh…sure? Yes. I'd love to," I bumble out like an

idiot and step closer to him. He smells fresh like lemons.

"I'm Liam," he says and extends his hand.

I wipe my hand on my yoga pants. Classy. "Jennifer. Nice to meet you."

We walk in silence for a bit until he points out the apartment he rented for the week, a recently renovated historic building.

"I watched them redo the warehouse and always wanted a peek inside. It's an apartment building now?"

"Well, lass come on in. I'll give you the grand tour. I'll put the kettle on, and we'll drink our cuppa here instead."

We pause in front of his place, and he waits for my answer. Will it be safe to step inside with him, a complete stranger? I reach toward his face and touch his light-brown hair falling into his eyes. Specks of gray fleck through showing his age.

With one touch from me, he releases his breath and leans toward me. "I'm chuffed. Wanted to chat you up for days now. Don't think I'm a wanker, but I hoped to see you every day on my walk. Planned my day around it after I saw you chatting to yourself with a cheeky smile on your face."

"Yes." I nod. We step inside a space with concrete floors. Sunlight pours in everywhere. The industrial modern design kept the exposed brick and old metal hardware. I walk around and notice him watching me, eyes glazed. He steps forward and grabs my waist.

"Yes, this." His lips dive onto mine before I respond. He kisses his way down my neck and backs me into the brick wall. "You smell like spring," he whispers between kisses. "I plan to find out how you smell everywhere. Work for you?"

I nod as he grabs my lips with his and yanks off my clothes. I stare down at my naked body. How did I end up nude in a stranger's apartment rental? His strong arms carry me through the loft as he caresses my breast. The sparse bedroom opens to the living area. He places me on rumpled sheets in his bed then stands back to examine me spread out before him.

"What a cracking beauty."

My heart beats fast. "I think I saw this movie," I choke out.

"Cheeky, I'm just a regular bloke from Manchester, England. Business consultant with Barclays. Loyal to Her Majesty. I married my best mate twenty-five years ago. Me wife knows I dabble with other lasses now and again when I travel. It's our agreement. She keeps a bloke on the side, too." He takes his clothes off and crawls up the bed. "You all right? If not, we can stop."

Not sure how to answer, my response comes out as a question, "Uh…are we good?"

He takes his time to kiss up my body, but his movements lack urgency. The slowness gives me too much time to think. Dean keeps popping up in my thoughts. I want Dean's body on mine, not Liam's from England.

I blurt out, "Uh, yeah, maybe work a little faster?" I can't find anything else to say other than hurry the fuck up.

"Sure then." His pace quickens, and he stops talking.

Quiet breathing overwhelms me in the otherwise silent apartment. Even the traffic noises outside dissipate. He must think the same thought because he jumps up and turns on the radio. Electronic dance music blares from the built-in house speakers. I giggle like a lunatic teenager from the incongruent scene set before me. "This music is ridiculous."

He turns back to bed, perhaps believing I enjoy his music choice, and shakes in a dance. His handsome body wiggles its tiny potbelly around, and I laugh more. He comes back to bed, places his long body right next to mine, and sings nonexistent words with the song on the radio.

"A cup of tea, his woman left him, and now he's a drunk…" Liam leans toward the strange.

He belts out the obnoxious made-up lyrics again. Song over, he returns to trailing sweet kisses up my legs. He worships my body as he climbs his way up using his tongue and lips to lead the way, licking and sucking. I watch him without moving, without giving back for a bit, and am mesmerized someone can be so artful with his tongue. This man knows how to seduce a woman with his lips, and he seems to care I'm satisfied.

"Ooohhh," I moan as he stops kissing my body.

"You all right with this?" he says asking for permission.

I nod my head yes. No woman in the universe would say no to this mind-altering kissing experience.

"I want to tell you up-front. I only snog. Bugger, I cocked up. Speak American now. I only kiss. I don't cheat by shagging."

This wakes me right up. His rhythmic tongue movement revved me up, but he only wants this? He recognizes my confusion and stops. His hand trails down my body catching in certain spots to caress my skin. He likes the curves and plays with the turns my body takes. His light touch arouses, creating goose bumps over my chest. He blows on my wet breast.

"I can tell you need this more often. Most women need adoration," he whispers as he ducks down suckling and swirling my nipple in his mouth. Kissing me again.

"Umm…mmm," I answer with an animal grunt attempting to understand the situation. His tongue works along my skin like a naughty massage.

He kisses between my thighs but quickly this time with an up and down motion. I moan from pleasure. A carnal freeness flows through me, but I don't climax. He slows down, rubbing our bodies together, and stops.

"You're a ledge. I'm knackered. I'll get you a cuppa," he says and bounces out of bed.

I don't know what to say. There are no words for what just happened. This is a super strange experience. I definitely don't want him to explain himself. I leave it alone and wait for my body's response.

He kisses me again, but in a platonic way this time. He leaves the room; I presume to put on a pot of tea as the faucet runs in the kitchen. I dress and exit the loft. My feet find the path home, and I laugh thinking about Liam. I text Anna.

—Holy taco, do I have a crazy story for you.—

****

Dean calls in the afternoon. "Hey, how are you? I wanted to check on you." My heart stops at his deep voice. The pit of my stomach turns in turmoil. Is it guilt over the Sexy Stranger?

His words register in my brain, and my mouth drops open. "Check on me about what?"

"I thought about you all day today. I know things are stressful, Jennifer, but if you need to talk, I want to listen. Call me. I'm here for you."

Did he really say he wants to help? Someone emotionally available and open makes my palms sweat.

Dean was only supposed to be someone to write about, a hookup, another dude on the checklist.

"I understand your feelings and am conflicted. I really care about you, but I also know this is a rough patch in your marriage. I don't want to make it harder on you. I can back off until you get things figured out," Dean says.

Someone, other than Anna, cares about me. Shit, Jake didn't even notice I fell off the rails. Jake lives on the opposite side of the emotional maturity scale from Dean. He would call Dean a pussy if he heard him talk like this. I change the subject and put Dean back in his place. "You thought about me today? Was I wearing clothes?" I shoot back at him in a silly, sultry voice. I won't let my guard down.

"Hey, now, you're not just sex to me. I can listen when you need me. Although, playtime is pretty damn fun, too." He chuckles on an exhale.

"Any chance we can sexy time play sometime today? I want to kiss something," I shoot back at him.

He laughs and sighs. "I can barely answer. You are so fucking sexy. Seriously, Jennifer, I want to touch you tonight. Your skin is so soft, and I can't stop thinking about you and your sweet little moans, but I have the kids and meetings all day today."

He has me. I want him to make me moan. Jake is gone only a few more nights. "Can't you get a sitter? Just for an hour? I can give you the name of one."

"Okay, yeah, just for an hour. Late though, after the kids go to bed."

"Great. Meet me out back again, our chair at nine forty-five. Remember to be quiet as a mouse. I'll tuck the kids in by eight p.m."

"See you then, sweetheart."

****

My hands curl around a warm silver travel mug of coffee as the wind blows puffs of cold air around the field. My hair blows in my face. I comb my fingers through to resettle it.

"Get the ball. Now. Go," a mom next to me screams standing from her folding chair.

My athletic kid runs fast with the soccer ball. "Kevin looks good on the field," a voice behind me says. "He's improved this year. Seems like a completely different kid from last season." I turn to find Dean looking down at me. "Mind if I sit on your blanket with you?"

Unsure how to answer, I smile as he sits. I glance around to make sure no one notices us or guesses what we've done together. Shit, I take a deep breath and inhale the fresh-cut grass of the soccer field. "Hi."

"Yay, you got this. Go Lions," another parent screams at the top of her lungs.

Dean flinches a little. "The parents are all so serious."

"I know. I think they forget it's just a game." Someone I recognize walks across the field. Shit, it couldn't be.

"So what do you think?" Dean asks.

"What?" No clue what he just said. I slip my sunglasses on and turn to the side. Fuck. Suit man from the coffee shop cannot be here right now. I squint in his direction and hope he doesn't see me.

"I asked about the game. What's the deal with these aggressive soccer moms?" he whispers, watching a mom next to us stand to get a better view of her kid.

"Here you are. Why didn't ya bring chairs? You know I hate sitting in the dirt. Damn, it's cold." Jake stands above me.

"What are you doing here?" I ask two octaves higher than normal.

"Thought I should come to one of his games before the season ends."

"Uhh…" I don't have a single thing to say other than cuss words.

"Dean." Jake frowns and sits next to him.

My gaze flicks back and forth between the two men. Shit. Fuck. Shit.

"Jake." Dean smirks at him. The obvious dislike swells around us. Both men stare at the field focused on the game.

"Yeah, go get it, son. You got this," Jake screams.

Dean catches my eye and lifts his eyebrows.

I stare at the field and across the way. Suit guy waves to get someone's attention. I check over my shoulder to see who he's signaling and pivot back toward the field. He waves more using both arms.

"Uh, Jennifer. I think the man over there wants your attention," Dean says poking me in the arm.

"What guy?" I search around the soccer parents next to us.

"No. Across the field," Dean says.

"Where?" I play stupid and take a sip of my lukewarm coffee.

"Jennifer. Right there. Look." Dean points at Suit Man.

"Do ya know him?" Jake asks.

"Nope. Never seen him in my life. He must think I'm someone else."

"Well, he keeps waving this way," Dean says.

"It sure seems like he knows ya," Jake mumbles under his breath.

"Hmmmmm…" I almost gurgle in my throat, trying not to choke.

"Jennifer. Will ya please wave back? This is getting embarrassing. Other people are staring at us now," Jake whispers at me through gritted teeth.

I turn to the field, smile across, and casually wave. Suit man salutes me with a huge grin and walks away with a small kid following way behind him. Shit. Fuck. Shit.

"Weird. People are so damn obnoxious," Jake says.

"Okay, I gotta…" Dean can't even think of an excuse to get up and leave, so he doesn't finish his sentence.

"See you," I say to Dean excusing him from this mess.

"Bye, Jennifer. See you later." Dean walks away without acknowledging Jake.

"Hate him. He is such an asshole," Jake says under his breath.

I text Anna.

—Where the fuck are you? The game started and I'm in hell.—

She doesn't answer so I stare at the phone for a solid minute.

She finally answers. *—Soccer hell?—*

I pivot to face Jake so he can't see me typing.

—Well, yeah, soccer hell but also all the men I slept with hell. Get here fast. I need you.—

She responds immediately. *—OMW—*

I turn and watch the game like it's the most important thing in the entire world.

Chapter Eighteen

Anna

I lean back on the faux leather sofa at Cynthia's with a glass of wine in my hand. It's my second, and we only started book club ten minutes ago.

Whatever. The place reeks of vanilla and cappuccino Scentsy. I'm the only one in the room not down with plug-in air fresheners. They make me sick and so does Cynthia's place. Everything is too perfect. She's created a suburban paradise with multiple layers of cream colors, accents of steel-gray and marine-blue like an HGTV show just threw up.

No trace of kids or her husband exists anywhere in the space. Well, I guess the wreaths on each of her two kids' bedroom doors count for something. A blue flower arrangement with Tonka trucks and blocks for the boy and a pink one with cutesy dolls for the girl.

When she showed them off earlier, I smiled with the others and said, "What a talent."

"When I saw it on Pinterest, I just had to make them. Don't you love the creativity?"

It turns my stomach. I twirl my hair and take a huge swig.

"Okay, ladies, next week is the art show. Should we all meet up there or go together?" Cynthia starts the discussion.

I glare at Jennifer across the room. She drops her eyes to her wine glass.

"What art show?" Rebecca asks.

The girl can't remember her last name. She stares at her own reflection in the big glass window and primps. She does this through every book club. I peer at Jennifer and shake my head. She smirks back.

"You know the one with Nathan's work. Baristo Nathan, from the coffee shop," Megan says.

"Oh, right. Yeah, let's go together."

Everyone else agrees.

"Well, what did you think of this month's novel selection? Reading it broke my heart," Cynthia continues.

"I just love how the husband is, like, so totally real in this book."

Damn, Rebecca always says the same thing for every single book. How did she end up in our group? She's Cynthia's neighbor, so I guess Cynthia tried being friendly. Twenty-year-old Rebecca's fake tan and huge rack remind me of a Barbie doll. Honestly, she exemplifies the trophy wife we secretly dread will replace us someday. Not to mention, she's dumb as a doorknob.

"And when he broke down at the death of their son, I fell apart," Cynthia says.

Everyone agrees. I nod. I didn't read the book. I don't even know why I came. I guess to escape home.

"I know, and shit, the guilt she feels is unbelievable. She'll never recover from the loss," Jennifer says.

"Well, it's her own damn fault, right?" Damn. Did I just say that out loud?

"I don't know. I really don't think she could change the situation," Megan says.

"There is always something you can do or not do." I swig back the rest of my wine.

"The son did die of cancer, right?" Tammy only reads the jacket cover and then talks about the book like she read it.

"Yes, he died of cancer. Not something you can really *do* anything about or fix," Jennifer says, trying to direct me with her eyes.

I can't help myself. I glare back at Jennifer and throw it at Tammy. "I know he died of cancer, Tammy. I read the book unlike you." Her eyes go wide. "We all know you never read the books. Why come and ask silly questions based on the back cover every month? I don't get it."

"Well." Tammy turns red and glances around.

Cynthia glares at me with narrow eyes. "Now, we understand Tammy's busy life. It doesn't matter if you don't always read the entire book. Everyone's welcome."

"Really?" Rebecca says, "My husband said I must read the whole book. He sets time aside for me to read each day." She adjusts her hair in the window reflection.

I wave my arms around. "Damn it, Rebecca. Of course, he sets a timer because you are a child who needs a babysitter. And stop looking at yourself in the window. It's a window, not a mirror. You primp through every book club."

Cynthia gets up. "Anna, I don't think you should talk to us this way."

"Cynthia, where's your real house with toys and

garbage and jelly stains? What do you do? Keep the kids and the husband in the garage all day? I don't understand it. It's not natural for anyone to live this way." I pick up the decorative pillows from her couch, throw them across the room, and stomp into the kitchen. Scuffles and soft whispers fill the house as the ladies replace Cynthia's precious cushions. Whatever.

Jennifer follows me. The book club continues talking, but long pauses break up the chatter. They want to figure out what the heck is wrong with me. Well, so do I, ladies. I slump down onto the terrazzo tile floor of Cynthia's kitchen and lean against her maple cabinetry on the far side of the island.

Jennifer sits in front of me cross-legged. She touches my hand. "What's wrong?"

I glare up at her. Tears stream down my face. "Damn it. This stuff is all your fault." My too loud whisper carries to the next room. "Why did you suggest all this stuff? You know I did *it* with four men other than my husband? Look at me. My life fell apart. I fell apart."

"My fault?" Her voice rises. "You are the one who said let's do it. I thought we both agreed. No emotions. No connection. Just hookups."

"Whatever. I said to write it, not do *it.* You're the one who said we needed to experience *it*."

"Shit. No one forced you to do anything. You made your own choices and so did I. Grow up and deal with the consequences." Jennifer rips her scarf off and throws it on the kitchen floor.

"Grow up? Your damn answer to everything. Well, we are damn grown-ups, and it's still a problem. Everything sucks: my marriage, my job, and my mothering skills. And what's your brilliant suggestion? Write a"—my voice lowers—"porno book. What happened to marriage counseling or changing careers or ask your doctor about antidepressants? That's normal best friend advice. I listened to you and now everything in my life's awful."

"I wasn't serious. I feel like shit, too." Her voice rises in the now silent house. The conversation in the next room halts. The book club ladies listen to every word. "You're the one who took this to a whole new level."

"Me. A whole new level? That's your department."

"My department? What the fuck do you mean?"

"Whatever, Jennifer. You know what it means. Like you did back in college. You always take things to a whole new level and push the boundaries. Always the life of the party but you never experience the consequences. You ruined everything in my life back then, too."

"Really? It's been over twenty years, Anna. You need to get over college."

I bite my lip and grit my teeth. "I was put on probation and lost my scholarship. My mom still brings it up every chance she gets. You wrecked my life. Damn it, you wrecked it again."

"I didn't make you do anything." Jennifer picks up her scarf and throws it around her neck. "And it's 'fuck' by the way. You fucked four guys, not did *it.* Your life is fucked-up. Stop talking like your fucking grandmother."

My face drops into my hands. I weep big, ugly sobs. After a bit, she moves closer and touches my chin. I stare up at her. She smiles weakly. I gaze into her brown eyes, and she stares back. I lean my face in close and kiss her lips. She pulls back with a red face. Damn it, what did I do? I stand and drop the wine glass. Red wine and crystal glass shatters on Cynthia's perfect kitchen floor as I run out of the house and away from my best friend.

****

After driving aimlessly for an hour, I sit in my car with the engine off in the parking lot of Nathan's coffee shop. I appreciate the chill in the air freezing my skin. My toes go numb. I want it to seep deeper inside me and take away any trace of Allessandro from my body. His scent lingers on my clothing, the same dirty clothes I wore on the plane and redressed in today.

My mind blurs and jumps from my time in Italy to Luke. The night after he picked me up from the airport, we fed the kids dinner and tucked them into bed. We were physically in the same room but not connected. Nothing's changed since. I think back to last night's bedtime conversation.

"You have the kids alone all week," Luke said. "The firm needs more time to prepare for a big case, so I will come home late most nights. I may even stay in the firm's apartment."

"You know it's parent-teacher conferences all day Thursday. I reminded you about it last week." I sigh.

Luke paused for a moment. "I can't on Thursday. There isn't any way I can miss work for the day."

"And what am I supposed to do? I can't do conferences with my own kids in the room." He didn't say anything. "I'll ask Jennifer to take them, but you must attend their conferences."

He pulled out his phone. "What time?"

"I signed you up at eight a.m. for Brooklyn and eight-thirty for Ben. You could be in the office by nine-thirty."

"Fine. I'll move things around."

"And your mom's birthday party on Sunday?"

"Crap. I forgot." We divided up the duties and went to sleep without a single kiss goodnight. We never talk about anything deeper than chauffeuring the kids to their activities. I don't even know if we could talk to one another as adults again. I want to tell him how unhappy I am. How much I miss us. Does he feel it too? Is he happy? Does he want us? Where did the young couple in love go, and can we find them again?

I stare at Nathan's apartment and hope he's alone. Minutes pass, and I picture him naked on top of me. I imagine Jay, the bouncer, *doing* me in the bathroom of C-20, and Allessandro's hands running over my breasts. I imagine the Frenchman in the airplane bathroom. My mind wanders back to Luke, the two of us in college, doing *it* in the back of his Buick. I wrap my thoughts around our wedding night, making love for the first time as husband and wife. I wipe a tear from my cheek. Damn it.

Nathan opens the back door of the coffee shop and locks it. I step out of my car.

"*Ciao*."

"Anna," he says with a smile to melt all others.

"I need to talk with you."

"Okay. Come on up."

I follow him to his apartment. He opens the door, and darkness surrounds us with the lights out and the shades drawn. I smell Chinese food before I locate the containers on the kitchen table by the door. Damn it.

Jessica. I start to speak, but his hand covers my mouth.

"Shhh." He puts his finger up.

A girl's long, loud moaning penetrates the room. A male voice joins hers. Their figures intertwine on the bed. Nathan pushes me against the wall.

"I'm glad you're here. I love to hear her fuck, but this is better," he whispers into my ear. His body pushes hard against me, and kisses line my neck. His tongue goes up and down and all around. I whimper.

"Shhh."

Damn it. This is weird, but their moaning turns me on.

"No, I'm here to talk," I say in his ear.

"Fuck now," he whispers back. I need to convince him not to put the painting of me in the show. Nothing is final with Luke, and I'm certain it will end if he finds out about the painting. "Talk later."

I crave sexual touch since returning from Rome. I want to free my overthinking mind, so I succumb. The weird complications of him and his girlfriend don't stop me. The endless thoughts in my mind go blank, and I focus on his touch, his manliness, his tongue on my neck, and my breasts. He pins me against the wall and rips off my clothing. I tear off his, and his girlfriend groans across the room.

He drags me to the bathroom but keeps the light off and the door open. Her screams pierce the apartment. A condom slides on, and he yanks me on top of him. The cold tile floor rubs against my legs. Nathan grabs my bottom and glides me back and forth. The pleasure builds.

He flips me over. I kneel on all fours. He rubs around but doesn't enter. He pushes in but too high.

I say, "Lower."

"No. Trust me." He pushes just a little in small thrusts until he enters completely. It hurts and vibrates with pleasure at the same time. I moan.

He laughs. "Shhh." He takes something from a box in the bathroom and turns it on. Buzzing hits my ear. Damn, he's got the place wired. After holding it on me for an instant, I orgasm.

Hands grab my breasts and pinch my nipples. He groans and collapses beside me as his girlfriend moans in the next room. Nathan kneels and shuts the door.

"She goes on forever. Even after the guy's done, she'll make him fuck her with his fingers or a dildo. Her sex noises amaze me."

"Yeah, I guess."

"Shhh, listen to her."

Soft voices murmur, "Time to go. My boyfriend will come back soon. Dude's got a gun, too."

He grins. "She loves scaring them." Clothing shuffles in the background as the guy scrambles to dress and slams the door.

Seconds later, Jessica stands there naked in the doorway with her perfect little body mocking me. "Oh, hey, middle-aged mom."

I hate this damn girl.

"Eggroll?"

"Fuck yeah." Nathan sits on the tile floor beside me. She brings the boxes of Chinese food and snuggles up to him, naked.

"Shouldn't we eat at the table or put some clothes on?"

"Yes, Mom, we should." She grins. "But we won't."

He laughs, too. What the heck did I get myself into? She gives me a pair of chopsticks, and to show I'm not some sort of stick in the mud, I start eating naked in the bathroom with some guy I just did *it* with and his girlfriend.

"Anna what did you want to talk about?"

"The painting. I wonder if it needs to be in the show. Maybe you could change the face, so it doesn't look exactly like me." There I said it.

"Can't," he says through a mouth full of noodles.

"Why?"

"Nathan sold it two days ago. It will be unveiled in the show first and then off to the new owner."

"Then you don't need it for the show?"

"It's an integral part of the show. The sexuality of women. Nathan must display it."

I hate having this conversation with her instead of him. He nods accepting her points and eating the food like a starved man.

"Please, it will completely wreck my life."

"Don't be so dramatic. It won't wreck your life," she says between bites of an eggroll.

"Please." I beg with my eyes.

She leans in and pinches my naked ass.

"What the heck?" I frown.

"Oh, you even sound like a mom. She is soft, isn't she?" She eyes me with the look of a seductress. I twirl my hair.

"F-you." Damn it, Jennifer was right. I can't even say the F-word. Whatever. She laughs at me, and I hit her tight, young bottom. I hate her.

"Oh, now this I like." He smiles, and his body rises to the occasion.

"I'm sure she won't want to fuck us. She's much too conventional, but it's why you like her. He described you as fucking his friend's cute mom. A fantasy for all boys at some point, but watching the friend's cute mom fuck your girlfriend is a new one, right?"

"Fuck, yeah. You always create fun fantasies." He leans in and kisses her like a high five for her sexual depravity.

Jessica puts down the food and leans her face in close to me. She goads me, playing. I want to prove her wrong. She pauses with her lips an inch from mine waiting for my response. I'm a little curious. He touches himself and moans. I can't help it. I move forward and kiss her. I rub my tongue against her eager mouth.

"No to down there," I say, making it final.

"Leave that to me." Nathan smiles.

She stands, takes my hand, and I follow her to their bed. We leave Chinese food all over the bathroom floor. It would be a lie if I said I didn't want to stop and clean the mess. She sprawls out on the bed and pats the mattress inviting me to her. We kiss. Her soft lips touch mine in the same way as other kissing but for the taste of fruity lip gloss. I touch her body and she mine, which sends a warm sensation between my thighs.

Nathan puts on a show-stopping performance. Sliding on a condom, he does her and pleases me before switching and *doing* me while attending to her needs. A vibrator buzzes. They must keep them everywhere.

His body thrusts into her while he holds the vibrator on me. She continues to kiss and stroke my body. I climax. She takes a while, and he *does* me while holding the vibrator on her. I fondle her body and kiss her neck until she screams in pleasure. She plays with him while he continues inside me. He screams louder than necessary.

What do their neighbors think of the noise from this apartment? It must sound like subscribing to porn radio.

He lies down between us, which is good because I still hate her. But F-her if she thinks I'm some old fuddy-duddy now.

"She is nice and soft to fuck like you said."

"F-you, I'm right here."

"Yeah, but it's fun to talk about you."

"Well, your boobs are small." A petty jab but all I can say because the girl is perfect otherwise.

"Yeah, but my ass is small, too."

"At least I have nice boobs."

"You do. But you have a big ass."

Nathan joins the battle. "It is the quandary of life, big ass, nice tits or small ass, small tits."

She sighs. "Only the fake ones have a small ass and big tits."

"Well, I guess you could buy fake ones?"

"No, and lose feeling? Never. Better to have small ones I can feel than fake ones. Besides, one day, I can get fat and have big ones and a big ass."

"If you're lucky, some people get fat and don't get big boobs," I add knowing full well even if she got fat, she'd still look perfect. *Whatever.*

"Shit, you're right. Quandary continues. Fuck, I'm hungry." She gets up to get more food.

"See. Told you she has ADHD. Can't sit still." He wraps his arms around me and snuggles me close.

She comes back with leftover eggrolls. “Look it’s tiny.” She pokes at his especially small tool.

He giggles. “Leave it alone.”

“It’s not often it gets dried out. You really liked it?” she says.

“I did.” He kisses me on the lips and smooches his naked body against mine.

He’s perfect but young, weird, and with Jessica. What did I do?

Chapter Nineteen

Anna

Damn. Why did I drive here of all places? Jay the Bouncer finally stopped sending his dirty tool pictures. I park crooked in two spaces but don't care. Whatever. After Nathan and Jessica, I hunger for more touch. My hands shake and my head spins. I stumble out of the car, not drunk, but I want to be.

Across the parking lot, Jay guards the entrance poker-faced. The heels of my boots click on the pavement as I walk toward him. This time I don't fall. I move into his space with only a breath of air between our bodies. Jay studies me and smiles. I bite my bottom lip.

He uses his headset to radio someone inside. "Carlos, I'm taking my break now."

"I need to get drunk." I twirl my hair.

"I can arrange that." He pinches my bottom.

The server drops a platter of shots in various hues and complexities onto our table. We sit next to each other in a corner booth. A weird space separates our bodies. I don't know if I should lean into him like a boyfriend or sit here like a friend. The dark room and loud music help me hide.

What do you say to someone twenty years younger than you? Especially when our only common connection is his expert johnson. Whatever. I say nothing, but he doesn't seem to care. His hand moves to my thigh. I sigh and sink into him. The warmth of his body fills my brain.

I pick an orange and red shot in front of me and point to the tray. He motions his head no. "Gotta work."

Damn, this is all for me. I tip back the shot and a burning sensation slips down my throat. I repeat the process with a clear liquid and again with glasses of blue and yellow. My body numbs. He must know it is enough alcohol because he takes my hand and leads me to the dance floor. He holds my bottom and presses me against his body. Dancing to the music makes the room spin. A song or two later, Jay leads me around the back of the bar and through the storeroom to an unlabeled door.

He opens it and turns on a light glowing red. The room, more like a closet, consists of a single bed with a fuzzy, lion print bedspread, and a small, wooden dresser. Some old glasses litter the dresser top along with a full ashtray. The place smells of beer and smoke, and I won't think of how many people did *it* here before us. Whatever.

Jay shuts the door with a distinct click as he locks it. I set down my purse, and he unzips my dress from the back. It falls gracefully to my feet. He leaves my boots on and pushes me to the bed. He pulls off his shirt and his muscles illuminate red, showing their full glory. Pants unzip and reveal his virility. They slide down and his shoes skid across the floor. He grabs a condom from the dresser drawer and slips it on his tool.

My Bouncer descends on me attacking my breasts with his hands and mouth. He slides my lace panties off. He shoves inside me. I moan. It's hard, fast, and desperate. I want more of his mouth on my lips. No, not his mouth. I don't want his lips on my lips. I want Allessandro on me, in me, with me. I squirm.

"What's wrong?"

"I just didn't…" I bite my bottom lip.

"Fuck." He stops and pulls out a vibrator and a bottle of tequila from a shelf. He pours some of the tequila over the vibrator. I guess to clean it? He takes a swig before passing me the bottle. I take a sip too and set it on the table. He licks my breast and flicks his tongue back and forth. I pretend he is Allessandro, but I can't. Their techniques are just too different. He is hard and fast where Allessandro was musical.

I think of Luke and the last time we had sex. It was robotic. Damn. My mind works against me, even this drunk. Sensing I won't orgasm anytime soon, he turns on the vibrator. The buzzing makes me think of Nathan, and when I first did *it* with him without the weird girlfriend. I felt like the most beautiful woman in the world. Then today. Damn it.

The vibrator sends a pulse through my body. I moan and my mind clears. I squirm as the pleasure grows, and I climax. The intensity leaves me breathless. It isn't like my time with Allessandro, which was caring and full of emotion. This is pure physical pleasure.

The vibrator falls to the floor and buzzes away adding to the din of the nightclub. Jay plunges into me with rough and emotionless movement, squeezing and thrusting his body against mine. The pleasure somehow numbs my pain.

He moans and pulls out. "Fuck me."

"I just did." He laughs, and I notice for the first

time his gentle eyes. He dresses, and I join him. I ogle his butt as he saunters toward the door in his tight jeans then returns to me, pressing his body into mine. Soft lips kiss mine for the first time tonight. Allessandro was all about my lips.

"Gotta work. Call you a cab?"

"Cab? Damn it. I need to get my car home, too."

"I'll take you and your car back at two. Then I can get a cab back here."

I bit my bottom lip. "Really? You don't mind?"

"No. Rest or come out and dance." His body wiggles in a little boogie.

He leaves. It's the most we ever said to each other. I sit down on the bed and touch nothing. My stomach turns glancing around the filthy room. I grab the pack of cigarettes from the top of the dresser. I light one and inhale. Damn.

What is wrong with me? I did *it* with two guys tonight. Well, three if you count Jessica. I guess she counts, so three people. And I kissed Jennifer, my best friend. She sat there with me, supporting me, and I put my lips on her full mouth. Painted red, I could taste her lipstick. She pressed back for a second, confused. I wanted to be close, but I didn't mean to come on to her. Damn, she might never talk to me again. What a mess.

I check the time on my phone—one a.m. An hour to wait. The sex sobered me up, and I don't want to wallow in my own thoughts in this filthy closet.

I smash the cigarette out in the full ashtray. The bartender notices me walk out of the storage room. I blush. Everyone knows what I, a married woman with kids, did with the bouncer in the storage room. Damn. Damn. Damn.

Not sure what to do, I stand outside beside the bouncer Jay for a while. I twirl my hair and make small talk.

"So have you worked here long?"

"No," he grunts.

"Are you in school?"

"No."

"Where do you live?"

"Anna." He peers into my eyes. "Every guy wants to think somewhere, somehow, in someplace, a woman is out there who just wants to fuck him. Nothing more. I always expected some young, college girl slumming it, but I was wrong. Happily wrong, because now I don't need to rush. I now know there are old chicks out there who just want to fuck, too. So please, don't fucking wreck this one fulfilled fantasy of fucking you just to fuck you."

I bite my bottom lip. "You know calling me old isn't sexy."

He winks at me and smiles. "Everything about you is sexy." He raises his eyebrows a moment and turns back into an expressionless bouncer.

"Okay. I'll wait in my car."

"Passenger side."

"Yep."

I sit in my car watching people leave the club in small groups, couples, or alone. Jay stays emotionless, opening the door and looking menacing. I picture him naked and remember our first thrilling night doing it with him in the bathroom. I flash to Nathan and his weird girlfriend Jessica. Should I be more concerned about doing *it* with three people tonight or that one of them was a woman? Damn it. No matter the original thought, it always runs back to Allessandro.

****

I startle awake at the taps on the glass beside me. It's Luke. Damn it. Where am I? I don't remember getting home or driving. No. No, wait. I'm on the passenger side of the car. Jay the bouncer brought me home. What does Luke know? I move to roll down the window, but the key isn't in the ignition, so it doesn't move. The key? Where's the damn key? In my hand. God help me. I put it in the ignition and push down the window button.

Luke glares at me. "Do I want to know?"

"No, you don't." He moves around the car to the driver's side and climbs in. An eerie light falls over our neighborhood. The clock in the car reads four thirty-two a.m. in glowing green.

"So," he says and waits. I'm glad he doesn't stare. I don't respond. I take a deep breath and inhale the putrid air freshener covering the old vomit smell in the car. What can I say? He passes me a shiny, gold iPhone I don't recognize. "I broke mine and took it to the Apple store after work. Insurance replaced it. The Apple genius synced my old phone to the new one. Except, he wasn't much of a genius and made a mistake. He synced your phone number from your account instead of mine."

My heart jumps. No. Damn. No.

"I didn't notice until after I put the kids in bed. I stayed up all night reading."

My stomach turns over. I force back the urge to hurl. My mind flashes through the texts to Jennifer, my God, and the naughty pictures from Jay I didn't erase. The photos from Rome of Allessandro and me. Damn, what else is on my phone?

He peers into my eyes. “Who the fuck are you? I thought you were my wife and the mother to our children.”

What can I say? He knows everything. There is no way to make this better.

“What? You have nothing to say? I don’t even get an explanation?” he asks.

“I…” I stumble over the words, “I don’t know what to say.”

“You blew up our whole fucking life and you don’t know what to say? If you wanted to get a divorce, you should have asked for one. Not do all this shit.” He gestures to the phone.

“I don’t want a divorce, but I’m not happy. I started writing and got carried away. But us…you and me, we haven’t connected for a long time. You’re never here. Even when you are present, you aren’t available. We don’t talk or make love or do anything anymore. I want things to be like before when we were in love.” I didn’t know until this exact moment the truth of my statement.

He takes back his phone and points to it. “These aren’t the actions of someone who wants *us* to connect or be in love.” He pauses. “You still want to be a mother to our kids, correct?” His eyebrows arch in question.

“Of course.”

“Fine then.” His eyes drop. “I’ll take the kids to school. You don’t look like you are in the position to drive anywhere. You probably should call in sick, again. I’ll pack a bag and go to my mother’s. I can’t be here with you.” His matter-of-fact emotionless voice cuts through me.

"Wait. Can't we talk about this?"

"I'll pick the kids up on the weekend." He stomps back to the house. What the heck did I do? I reach for my phone to call Jennifer. My head hits the dashboard as I remember our fight. Damn, I tried to kiss her last night. Tears roll down my cheeks. What have I done? I slump in the passenger side of my car completely frozen.

Chapter Twenty

Jennifer

With a cup of black coffee in one hand and a Motrin bottle in the other, I suck down two tablets to get rid of this headache. Hungover, my head throbs from last night's lack of sleep, three glasses of red wine, and a few shots of vodka. Holy taco, it's a deadly combination. Not a great day for parent-teacher conferences. I will plop them in front of a screen to survive. "Mom, more cereal please." Children demand from the kitchen table.

I pour my kids their Annie's Fruity Bunnies and berate myself for spending one more steamy night with Dean. "Yeah, let's try and play the quiet game this morning. Whoever is quiet the longest gets ice cream later," I bribe.

"What about the soccer game later today?"

"We will skip the soccer game and eat the biggest ice cream ever. Go get a bowl of cereal and watch cartoons for now."

"We can eat in the family room?"

"Yes. Just be quiet, please." All my rules and schedules dissipate before my eyes. I slump down on the couch with my coffee.

I tried to tell Dean there would be no more sex, but he is so difficult to turn down. Every time I say no, he charms me, and I change my mind. Then I invite him over for sexy playtime or show up at his house for a massage. It's sick. Officially, all personal boundaries with him are gone, and I like the tingling of his touch. Being with him is so much fun, so easy. Granted, Dean exudes sex, has no complications, and likes me so I can't say no. He is gorgeous on top of it all. Middle age suits him. Every time I see him, I want to crawl up him naked.

After sexy time with Dean last night, I couldn't sleep. The pit of dread in my stomach grew larger thinking of the disaster I made with Jake, Dean, and now Anna. What a mess we made of our friendship. Last night, I drank vodka shots alone, got drunk, and wrote three chapters of the porn book. I certainly dance with my own form of crazy now.

"Hey, kids, I'm home," Jake yells throughout the house banging the garage door closed behind him, home from yet another business trip. I uncurl from the couch and place my trashy novel face down so no one will see the naughty cover. I pause when I realize he said, "Hey kids," purposefully not including me. Ugh, shit.

"Hi, Dad." The kids yell back from the family room, and I vaguely remember the days when they rushed into his arms screaming, "Daddy, Daddy, you're home." These teenagers are in a different space from those toddler years.

I walk into the kitchen to find Jake standing there in his golf clothes waiting for someone to greet him. "I guess they don't care I'm home?" he says to me with a strange, blank face.

They would also react calmly to a divorce if we

split, another different reaction than a small child's. Where did the divorce thought come from?

"Did you have a nice trip?" I ask and fake a smile.

"Not really."

"Oh? Why not?

"The trip was fine. All business. But I gotta interesting text late last night, almost this morning really. Not thinking straight since I received it."

"Yeah, who from? Is everything okay?" Fuck. Maybe someone texted Jake about my extracurricular activities?

"Everything is definitely not okay." His eyebrows raise up, and his face reddens. I know his angry face well. Shit. Fuck. Shit.

"Who was the text from, Jake?" I take a small step back.

"Luke."

"Luke? As in Anna's Luke?"

"Yep. One and the same."

"Is Anna okay?" What the fuck happened? Did Anna lose it completely? A tremor in my stomach clenches. I should have reached out to her by now.

"I really, really, *really* don't think Anna is okay," Jake whispers through gritted teeth.

"Shit, what did the text say, Jake?" My breathing speeds up, and my legs wobble.

"It said, 'You better talk to your wife and whatever you do, don't sleep with her. You might catch something.' " I gasp and grab my chest. How could Anna have been so careless?

"So, wife," Jake mumbles into my ear. My body trembles. "Can we talk for real once I put my bags away? Maybe a walk around the block?" He doesn't look at me or wait for an answer as he leaves the room.

"Sure." My voice cracks. "Let me go put on some tennis shoes and tell the kids we'll be back soon," I say to an empty kitchen and collect myself. My mind races for a story to explain things.

We lock the front door in silence.

"I feel sick all the time." Jake spews once we walk a few steps away from our house. "I know this might be the whole cliché middle age man thing, but I expected more. I hate my life, and truthfully, I resent and hate ya. And the messed up thing is, my unhappiness has absolutely nothing to do with Luke's text."

I don't know what to say. "Oh?" I stare at him to stop my body from shaking as we walk. I wobble, unsteady on my feet.

His gaze squints at the pavement. "Look, I know ya screwed around or had an affair or something messed up. But to be honest, I really don't care, and it's the worst part of this situation. I don't care. At all."

"Jake…" I start to speak, but he interrupts me, his voice gravelly.

"I love the kids. I really do. They amaze me. I hate living in this Groundhog Day existence. I hate my job. I don't feel connected to ya. I really don't even like ya anymore, at least not enough to be married to ya. I'm glad ya screwed around on me. I can finally make a change. Your infidelity forced me to get out of this horrible marriage."

"You don't like me? You hate me?" is all I can say in response. "What do you mean?"

"I really don't," Jake says overly calm now. "I really don't like ya at all. You always want to go out and try new things. It's too much. I stopped loving ya years ago."

"What about the kids?" My head spins. How can this happen, and why get angry with him about it? This break up is exactly what I want. I don't like him either, but the words hurt.

"It's really amazing we have such great kids." He walks faster.

"Jake…" I start again. Shit. My fists ball up, and blood rushes to my face.

"Before I even got Luke's insane text, I spent the entire week figuring out what to say to ya to get out of this marriage. I know ya really aren't happy either. We both are stuck together on this life plateau somehow. I don't want a divorce from the kids. God no. Never. I really love them. I feel trapped and want out of the relationship. I really hate being with ya. I want a divorce."

I stop walking, my shoulders relax, and my fists unclench. There is no reason to be upset with him. He isn't happy and neither am I. "A divorce? A divorce."

"I know it sounds mean and ugly. Don't worry, I haven't lawyered up already. I just started thinking about it. Though I bet Luke would take my case in a second. I really don't want to be married to ya anymore. This isn't the life I want, Jennifer. I need out. Now."

"Okay," I mumble. "Is there someone else already?" I want to kick myself. Like I can say anything.

Jake stops walking in the middle of the street and turns to me. "Jennifer, isn't that my line? Aren't you the one who already screwed around?"

I grab his hand. "Jake, I'm sorry. I shouldn't ask obnoxious questions. I truly am sorry we didn't work out. I agree with you. You're right." He shakes me off him. "I don't know how to make us fit together anymore. I honestly don't know how we let it get so bad. One minute, we planned a life together and made beautiful babies. The next minute, this. Now, I prefer to hole up alone in my office and write than hang out and watch TV with you. I'm sorry things got so miserable. Ugh, I don't know how we got here."

We continue walking in silence for a bit when he says, "Look, let's not be shitty with this breakup. Divorce can be nasty. I don't want the ugliness. Let's remember how much we both love the kids. I really want them healthy throughout this whole life change. I don't want to get caught up in the custody and money of it all. Let's make them our number one priority. Can we be civil about this whole thing? Can we do the best things for the kids without screwing one another over?"

I sigh, and tears well up in my eyes. "Yeah, Jake. We can." I turn to hug him, but he steps away. "Civil sounds good."

****

Anna

I wipe off spilled curry sauce from the kitchen stove and stack the last of the dinner plates into the dishwasher. I shake the rice cooker over the sink. It rattles like a maraca. Brooklyn wanted to help make dinner tonight and put the rice and water into the rice cooker without the bowl. Now, grains of rice stick in the motor and scatter out of the machine and all over the kitchen. I keep shaking, but it's a futile task. Whatever. My phone buzzes in my pocket. I pull it out and read a text from Jennifer.

—We got an agent.—

It's the first text from Jennifer since I kissed her at book club. Damn it, my boundaries were so out of control. Not anymore. Since Luke left me, I'm one hundred percent mom all the time and haven't missed a single day of work. I put on a happy face and get through the routine. It's the evenings like tonight when I suffer.

I reply. I thought she'd given up on the writing project. I did.

—What?—

Her reply comes in an instant.

—I shopped out our manuscript. Sent a couple of queries to agents with the first three chapters and one of them called this morning. They read the entire manuscript and sent an offer for representation.—

—Wow, brilliant. You finished it?—

I don't know if I'm happy or sad. I destroyed my life for a novel. At least now it will be a published book, a damn erotic book, but a book, nonetheless. I text her again.

—How are you?—

—I'll put the paperwork in your mailbox.—

I get nothing else back from her. It was wrong to blame her for everything falling apart. I destroyed it myself. Bringing up our college fight didn't help the situation either. Kissing her was the last straw. I put the phone down and shake the rice cooker some more. A few grains fall on the tile floor.

I give up on cleaning the kitchen and change out the laundry before heading to the family room. I move the half-rotten banana peel aside and sink into the couch cushions. A flip through Netflix yields nothing interesting.

I scroll through my phone and find endless dribble on Facebook. I click 'like' for a colleague's new baby picture and guilt for not taking the time to write congratulations invades me. A reel of bad behavior leading to the end of my marriage spins through my mind. It's time to text Jennifer again. Our conversation remained one-sided before today's publishing text from her with only a series of texts from me.

—Ciao.—

—Jennifer, can we talk?—

—Please, just give me a couple of minutes.—

—I'm so sorry. I shouldn't have said those things.—

—You are all I have left. I am an idiot.—

—I miss you.—

—Please forgive me.—

I let out a sigh. I lost her in my life, too. I wrecked everything. I pulled apart my family, my marriage, and lost my best friend in a matter of months. I sink further into the couch and tears pour down my cheeks. I close my eyes and wake with the dog licking my face.

I pick up my phone and look at the time, 2:01 a.m. I try one last text.

—Middle-aged, chubby mom cries herself to sleep because she F-ed up, literally and figuratively. Plans to meet her best friend of twenty years at the little coffee shop on Wednesday at two p.m. to make amends. She promises not to kiss her. Your turn. Ciao.—

I hit send and drag myself to bed.

Chapter Twenty-One

Anna

The place overflows with couples in designer suits and shiny cocktail dresses. Waiters in black and white tuxes travel the crowd with tiny finger foods and champagne flutes.

I didn't expect this decadence. I pictured an abandoned warehouse with young, hipster dudes in full beards and flannel shirts talking about art while listening to the newest of Tulsa's underground bands. Oh, and they'd drink craft beer, too. It's the complete opposite scene though with older couples reeking of money serenaded by a stringed quartet. Whatever.

The press floats around the room with oversized cameras. Society magazines take photos of Nathan and some old bitty. Damn, he looks good tonight in tight jeans and a silk shirt with the top buttons open revealing a hint of his hard body underneath. He dazzles his audience with his charm, sex, and talent. I don't see Jessica, thank God. I can't imagine how he kept her away from all the excitement. Maybe they broke up?

I stand in the crowd not knowing what to do or say and twirl my hair. I take an offered flute of champagne and move through the room sipping it. The bubbles hit my nose. I stop in front of a painting of a vajayjay. I wait a moment and pretend to admire it. Inside, I focus on breathing steadily to keep from turning red. At any moment, the next painting will be me naked and masturbating. Damn it.

I shake in front of a portrait displaying a young, blonde woman lying on a bed. She rubs her perky breasts with a come-hither expression of a pure sexy pinup.

"Obvious, isn't it. What you would expect from a sex picture? That's what makes this show so unique. The artist is a young man who visualizes sex everywhere and in everyone," an older gentleman beside me says. His red bow tie gleams under his unshaven face.

"I haven't seen the rest."

"Well, you're in for a treat. The best one reveals a middle-age woman masturbating, the turning point in the collection from the young sexy toys to the sexuality of real women. It's the mothers who birthed babies and suckled them on their teats taking the spotlight in this show."

Damn it. I turn red. Why the heck does this sexually enlightened baby boomer keep talking to me? He cocks his head and examines me closer.

"It's you, isn't it?"

"No." My hands shake so much I nearly drop the champagne.

He grabs my hand and turns toward an older woman his age with big round glasses and long gray hair. "Martha, look who I found. It's her, isn't it?"

"Yes, it is." She peers at me through her owl eyes.

Now, my face turns beet red.

"Oh, what did you do, Albert? You upset the poor

dear."

"I didn't do anything wrong. I merely recognized the muse of the painting, the star of the show."

I back away.

"You scared her off." She says as I run through the crowd.

I don't want to be recognized and don't know why I came tonight. I should go home, but since Luke left all I do is stay home in isolation. He takes the kids every weekend, and I watch TV on the couch. I work, clean, or sleep. I'm single and doing lots of nothing with my newfound freedom. When I received the invitation in the mail for the show opening, I had to see the painting responsible for destroying my life.

Who was the bold woman who did *it* with random strangers and flew to Rome on a whim? Not me. Not me anymore.

I turn and find an eight-foot, larger than life portrait of me masturbating half-naked. I didn't see the finished work, just the sketch and color mock-up. My mouth drops open, and I freeze surrounded by people glaring at my naked body. I fight the urge to shout at the woman in the painting to put on some damn clothes.

The small, red tag beside the painting reads, "Sold." I lift the tag wanting to know how much I sold for in paint—fifty-four thousand dollars. Damn, no wonder Nathan refused to take it out of the show.

"I don't think he will work as a baristo any longer. All the paintings sold," says a familiar voice. "Were you wanting to buy?"

"No, I'm not in the market. You?" I turn to the man beside me, hoping he won't ridicule me. Luke faces me. My heart stops.

"No, I let the real thing go." He catches my eye.

"Oh?" I bite my lower lip.

He sips his champagne. "Yes, a beautiful, sexy woman I neglected and stopped taking care of properly."

"I'm sure she bears some responsibility." I gaze down at my black leather boots from Rome.

"Maybe." He touches my hand ever so slightly.

I let out a breath of air. "I mean if she's up here on the wall naked, she obviously didn't commit to the relationship."

"A fair assumption, but I wasn't committed either. Though I didn't show this much flair." He gestures to the painting. "She had style. If she planned an affair, it would involve something dramatic like this, not fooling around with the secretary."

"The secretary?" I scrunch up my nose and picture Luke's secretary, a round woman about seventy with eggshell-blue hair.

"Not mine but my partner's secretary. Are the details important?"

"I guess they aren't now." I grip the champagne glass. "How long?" I stare directly into his eyes to suss out the truth.

"Six months or so." He pauses. "I looked for excitement but lost the most interesting woman I'll ever know." His head drops.

My tone turns harsh. "Remember what you said in the car. I thought you didn't know who the F she was anymore."

"I was hurt and judgmental. I never expected her to mess around—"

"But why wouldn't she if you were involved in an

affair for six months? You expected her to be the dutiful wife and mother all the while you're *doing it* with some secretary at your office? So all those long nights working, the weekends away, and all the complaints about the firm pushing too hard, you were really with her?"

"Yes." He focuses on his champagne. "I messed up."

"And then you let her think this disaster was all her fault?" My voice cracks. "Acting like she was the one to blow up the marriage and family and all the while it was you?"

"You're right." He peeks at me, tears forming at the corner of his eyes. "I wrecked everything and lost her." Reflected in his eyes, I recognize my own deep regret and futile wishes to turn back the clock.

I touch his cheek. "She probably lost something, too."

His sexy, long lashes flutter as his eyes meet mine. "Did she? Looks like she found herself. Like she took on life and lived it."

"She did something but ended up alone and full of regret."

He turns toward me. "Yeah, what do you think she regrets?"

"Hurting those she loves and losing him."

He steps closer. "Is there another choice where she doesn't lose him?"

"Yes." I inch toward him.

He leans in, and I inhale his scent. His touch brings familiar comfort and excitement, too. His lips touch mine, warm and soft. It blazes through my whole body. Not smooth like Allessandro, random like the

Frenchman, rough like Jay, or sensational like Nathan. Yet it's sexy and something more.

It holds life together, history, family, promises, and love. The deep kiss tingles in my toes because I love this man and have loved him for over a decade. The kiss reaches deep inside me. Our love remains true even if it won't sell in a porn book.

We walk out of the gallery hand in hand, and he drives me home to our house where we do *it* like we'd never done *it* before. This time it is worthy of a porn book, but damn it, that's private.

****

Jennifer

I walk around the house with a stick of incense in my hand and think about the changes over the last few weeks. The smoke billows out behind me in the quiet, empty house. The kids sleep at Jake's new bachelor pad a mile away this weekend. I want to call and check on them but don't. They seem well considering the circumstances, and it will only interrupt their new routine with their dad.

I grab a blanket and curl up on the couch to check my emails. The first message from our agent requests some small edit changes. The book with Anna is completed and waits to be sold to a publishing company.

My next email is from a new client with a brochure copy edit to fix. I glance through it. I built up a small business of freelance ghostwriting gigs for corporate bigwigs not wanting to write their own annual reviews or blog posts. I ran into Suit Man on the soccer field again and he introduced me to some colleagues. I won't get rich this way, but it's enough until I find something permanent.

Jake pays more child support than required by the state so the kids and I will be fine. Anything extra can go in their college savings account. I toss my phone on the couch and sink further into the cushions with my notebook computer and planner on my lap. The sofa lures me into a nap instead of work. I doze off for a few minutes when my cell phone beeps with a text from Dean.

—You free?—

Do I want to answer? A flash of heat hits me. I lie down on the cushy sofa and type.

—I am working.— I lie.

—I want to see you, Jennifer. Coffee? Tea? Wine? Dinner?—

I don't answer for a bit. I type an answer but delete it. It pings again from Dean.

—A walk in the woods? Skate park? Visit the trash dump? Recycle center?—

I pick up the phone and stare at his picture before pushing the call button. It rings once.

"Jennifer, do you need me to sing? I got a Lionel Richie number all lined up." I almost see his smile teasing me through the phone line.

"Hey, no song needed but I want you to work on your repertoire. Maybe expand into this century at least?"

"Got it. New Directions next time?"

I laugh. "You mean One Direction and no. They are a dead band already."

"Huh?" Dean's voice questions, surprised. "Guess I can't keep up."

I giggle again. "It's hard as they change like the wind. I guess you could go old school. Just no more Lionel."

"Can I talk you into meeting me tonight? I won't sing." I pause and listen to his breathing through the phone. "I feel the trepidation through your silence. We don't have to go to the trash dump."

I sigh into the phone a little too loud. Are we on the same wavelength? "Dean."

"No, wait. Don't say it. Hear me out. Okay? I know things seem crazy for you right now. I remember how I felt right after my divorce. I was a mess and felt like a complete failure even though I wanted the divorce as much as she did. I get it, Jennifer."

"Yeah?"

"But listen, this isn't a proposal, or a request to go steady, or become my girlfriend. I'm not even sure what word to use." He laughs and it makes me smile. "I want to take you out to dinner, in public. There doesn't need to be anything else, just a meal shared between two good friends. If it eventually turns into something more, I won't lie, I will be thrilled. But I don't want to push you."

"Real nice of you to say, Dean." My heart physically hurts as I say this.

"So dinner? Tonight? No singing. Please?" he says with hope in his voice.

I sigh loud into the phone. "I don't know. I kinda like your singing."

"So yes, to dinner?"

"It doesn't seem like a good idea right now," I warn.

"Okay, I'll back off. I get it. I do, but if you change

your mind, I'm here and still your friend. I like you, Jennifer."

Well, shit. "Okay, how about pizza out? Nothing too sexy time or date like. Can we go out on a friend date and do nothing but talk and eat some dinner? I need a friend. And maybe you can sing some Dylan."

"Anything you need. I'll pick you up at seven."

"No, wait. I'll meet you. Can't take the chance of being alone in the car with you. Mariano's at seven?"

"If you insist. See you then."

"And Dean, thank you for understanding."

"No problem. I can't wait to see you tonight."

After putting my phone on the coffee table, I turn to my computer. Getting back into the writing brain is a challenge, but I boot it up anyway. Sensual memories of my evenings with sexy Dean come flooding back. Far from platonic, but he wants to be friends now. Is he real? My face burns thinking about him and the things we did together. I can't convince myself to stay away, even if I try. He is too perfect to pass up.

****

Anna

On Wednesday afternoon, I arrive at our little coffee shop hoping Jennifer will meet me. The usual suspects, college students and hipsters, sprawl out across the small tables. I order a lavender tea and slide into a 1950's style kitchen chair. Soft jazz plays in the background.

Jennifer and I haven't spoken or texted since her message about the agent. She left contract paperwork in my mailbox offering representation. I signed and FedExed it back. She didn't respond to my plea for a coffee date. I don't know if she will show.

The bell to the shop dings. I turn, but it's some college kid with a laptop under one arm and a reusable coffee cup in the other.

My head drops to the table. This whole thing is such a mess.

"May I sit?"

My mouth drops open as I glance up at Jennifer. "Yes, please." She plops down and stares at me. She looks good, maybe even happy. My eyes widen. "I'm so sorry. I know none of this is your fault. I fell apart." I take a deep breath and fumble with my teabag.

"I'm sorry, too. We screwed up. We encouraged one another to do this insane writing project with sexy benefits."

"Yeah, we are evil accomplices, but I wouldn't have done any of it, if I had been happy with my life."

"No, me neither." We fall silent for a few minutes before she says, "Are we okay?"

"Yes. Friends forever." A wave of relief washes over my body in a warm tingle. I smile at her. She nods back to me. "Thank God, because you're all I've got. I messed up at book club."

"Yes, you did. It was epic."

"Plus, the painting limited all other social places I can frequent. Everyone we know saw it."

Jennifer smirks, "Including Luke?"

"Yes, but it kinda worked out." I bite my bottom lip. "So apparently he did his partner's secretary for six months."

"Holy shit taco."

"It's obvious now when I think about it. Why would a partner at the firm suddenly work like a first-year associate with constant late nights and weekends? The emotional distance and the lack of sex now make sense. So we both messed up big time. Though he said I did it with more flair."

"Ha, you did. You guys good now?"

"Define good?" I shrug my shoulders. "We're trying. We schedule two standing dates a week. We take dance lessons at the school you wrote about for one date, and the other is dinner out, somewhere we can talk. We might go to counseling. We also do *it* regularly again." A flush of red hits my face. How can I feel embarrassed about sex now after what I did and wrote? "It will take time to trust each other. How about you and Jake?"

"We're over. You know, he's an asshole, but we want to take care of the kids together. Neither of us wants an ugly divorce, even though our marriage sucked."

"Good then?" I'm not sure how to respond and twirl my hair.

"I don't know if he's always acted like an asshole or if our marriage made him into one. His anger turned into resentment. We stopped loving each other a long time ago. We both agree there is no point in staying together. His anger wasn't good for the kids. Divorce releases him from me, so yeah, I feel good."

"What about Dean?" I flash her a look.

Her eyes sparkle. "We plan to date but no sex for a while. I think I need to give the relationship a chance instead of fucking outside in the dark. I don't know what will happen between us, but I like him. A lot. But with the pending divorce, I'm in a super, messy place right now."

"What about getting work?"

"Yeah, I sort of got a writing job. It's freelance, but it pays well. Who knew I could land something after all these years not working?"

"I did."

"Yes, you did. Thank you for believing in me. I will need to get something stable eventually. Jake's got an apartment. I plan to stay in the house for a while. We want to share custody and divide everything fairly. It's very adult of us. Our divorce will end up way better than the marriage. Plus, he is super involved with the kids like never before. The kids seem happy. I guess they were sick of the fighting, too."

"I'm glad." I reach across the table and grab her hand. "You deserve this." My eyes drop. "I'm sorry about the kitchen floor situation. I don't know why I did that."

She squeezes my hand back. "Don't be sorry." She winks. "I know it's because I'm hot."

"Whatever." I laugh and drop her hand. "Shall we play? Him in the corner."

She says, "Easy one. Math grad student who frantically finishes his thesis while drinking too much coffee. Pays extra for late-night sex on the washing machine at his apartment's laundromat. Loves his mom and hotdogs. Best friend is his cat, Mildred. Your turn, the server." She raises her eyebrows.

"Oh her?" I say. "She works here with her lifetime best friend. They have big dreams for their lives, but they don't always make great choices."

Jennifer leans over and gives me a hug. "No matter what comes next, it will be better together."

About the Author

Anna and Jennifer are writing partners, parenting conspirators, and friends.

~*~

Visit Jennifer and Anna at
www.minivanaffairs.com

Also Available
from The Wild Rose Press, Inc.
and major retailers.

Surprise Me Again

By Anita Kidesu

Charged with trespassing and indecent exposure on Erik Stenson's private beach, Carson and Josie Sandberg return to South Padre Island to attend the court hearing. However, their reunion with Erik is not what they expected. An invitation for a drink turns into a weekend of passion that fulfills fantasies and leaves all parties wanting to explore more than bedroom bliss. Will time, distance, and family issues stand in the way of a relationship, or will they be surprised again?

Also Available
from The Wild Rose Press, Inc.
and major retailers.

What Wouldn't I Do

I Do Book Two

By Allie Fisher

My name is Alana Reed Master…

Doting wife and stay at home mom, that's what I was, desperately in love with my husband, a man whose bedroom eyes matched his bedroom expertise. A single mom when we met, I fell hard and never looked back until the day he asked me for a legal separation. He won't stop at divorce. He wants my girls, my home, and my life. And Dane Masters always gets what he wants.

I never expected a man like Sam Kealoha to enter my life. Recovering from his own heartbreak, he's got the body of a Polynesian God and a primal protectiveness that is sexy as hell. He's the man of my dreams, but I can't keep him. Now I'm forced to make choices that betray my heart while contemplating something I never thought I would do—get rid of my husband.

www.ingramcontent.com/pod-product-compliance
Lightning Source LLC
La Vergne TN
LVHW050623100826
845148LV00011B/1713

* 9 7 8 1 5 0 9 2 3 4 7 6 9 *